Cambridge Elements

Elements in the Gothic
edited by
Dale Townshend
Manchester Metropolitan University
Angela Wright
University of Sheffield

THE ETERNAL WANDERER

Christian Negotiations in the Gothic Mode

Mary Going
University of Sheffield

Shaftesbury Road, Cambridge CB2 8EA, United Kingdom

One Liberty Plaza, 20th Floor, New York, NY 10006, USA

477 Williamstown Road, Port Melbourne, VIC 3207, Australia

314–321, 3rd Floor, Plot 3, Splendor Forum, Jasola District Centre, New Delhi – 110025, India

103 Penang Road, #05–06/07, Visioncrest Commercial, Singapore 238467

Cambridge University Press is part of Cambridge University Press & Assessment, a department of the University of Cambridge.

We share the University's mission to contribute to society through the pursuit of education, learning and research at the highest international levels of excellence.

www.cambridge.org
Information on this title: www.cambridge.org/9781009517102

DOI: 10.1017/9781009151412

© Mary Going 2024

This publication is in copyright. Subject to statutory exception and to the provisions of relevant collective licensing agreements, no reproduction of any part may take place without the written permission of Cambridge University Press & Assessment.

When citing this work, please include a reference to the DOI 10.1017/9781009151412

First published 2024

A catalogue record for this publication is available from the British Library

ISBN 978-1-009-51710-2 Hardback
ISBN 978-1-009-15342-3 Paperback
ISSN 2634-8721 (online)
ISSN 2634-8713 (print)

Additional resources for this publication at www.Cambridge.org/Going

Cambridge University Press & Assessment has no responsibility for the persistence or accuracy of URLs for external or third-party internet websites referred to in this publication and does not guarantee that any content on such websites is, or will remain, accurate or appropriate.

The Eternal Wanderer

Christian Negotiations in the Gothic Mode

Elements in the Gothic

DOI: 10.1017/9781009151412
First published online: December 2024

Mary Going
University of Sheffield

Author for correspondence: Mary Going, m.going@sheffield.ac.uk

Abstract: *The Eternal Wanderer: Christian Negotiations in the Gothic Mode* provides new ways of reading the Gothicisation of the Wandering Jew. It argues that early Gothic writing conjured iterations of this figure that reimagine and revise him, adding Gothic layers to a popular Christian myth that refuses to die. Drawing on the work of Carol Margaret Davison, Lisa Lampert-Weissig and Galit Hasan-Roken and Alan Dundes, whose studies trace the myth's development across history, folklore and literature, this Element studies the figure as an antisemitic, palimpsestic Derridean spectre and establishes early Gothic writing as a significant development in his continued spectral existence. By reading the production of the Wandering Jew in conversation with his historical and theological contexts, and employing theoretical traditions of spectralisation according to Jacques Derrida and Steven F. Kruger, this Element provides a dedicated account of Gothic iterations of this figure and examines its alchemical, Faustian and theological figurations.

Keywords: Wandering Jew, Gothic, Christianity, Protestant, folklore

© Mary Going 2024

ISBNs: 9781009517102 (HB), 9781009153423 (PB), 9781009151412 (OC)
ISSNs: 2634-8721 (online), 2634-8713 (print)

Contents

1 Introduction: Mythic Beginnings and the Spectre of the Wandering Jew   1

2 Alchemical Reproductions: *St. Leon* and *St. Irvyne*   18

3 Faustian Incarnations: *Melmoth the Wanderer*   29

4 Theological Transformations: *Salathiel*   40

5 Conclusion: Gothic Legacies and Resurrections from *Dracula* to *Melmoth*   51

Bibliography   59

1 Introduction: Mythic Beginnings and the Spectre of the Wandering Jew

Continually appearing and reappearing across Europe, the Wandering Jew emerged from Israel after the resurrection of Jesus Christ and has been wandering the globe ever since. Or so the story goes. This story is in fact an apocryphal addition to the Passion narrative that chronicles the eternal wanderings of a Jewish figure throughout history after he is cursed and is unable to die, at least until the prophesied End Times. Though perhaps not well known today, he is a notable archetype of explicitly Jewish identity tied to the supernatural who gained prominence within Gothic fiction following his brief but striking inclusion in Matthew Gregory Lewis's *The Monk* (1796). The figure has appeared frequently in fiction, folklore and Gothic tales, through which Jewish identity is typically constructed by non-Jewish writers who ventriloquise a Jewish voice (for a list of texts that feature the Wandering Jew, please see the supplementary table that is included with this Element). Created in part to serve as witness to Christianity's central narratives of the Passion and Resurrection, the Wandering Jew also functions as a Jewish Other representative of a Christian desire to convert Jews to Christianity. Essentially, he is a Derridean spectre: as the figure has been conjured and re-conjured, he is retroactively inserted into the very stories his existence is designed to substantiate. Owing to the nature of oral traditions, the tale's origins may never be uncovered – he is, after all, absent from the Gospels, the New Testament or contemporaneous historical accounts. The Wandering Jew is, then, a later invention, existing only as a spectral presence within the Passion story as he is repeatedly conjured in stories, folklore and legends.

In *Specters of Marx*, Derrida asserts that

> The production of the ghost [...] is effected, with the corresponding expropriation or alienation, and only then, the ghostly moment *comes upon* it, adds to it a supplementary dimension, one more simulacrum, alienation, or expropriation. Namely, a body! In the flesh (*Leib*)! For there is no ghost, there is never any becoming-specter of the spirit without at least an appearance of flesh, in a space of invisible visibility, like the dis-appearing of an apparition. For there to be a ghost, there must be a return to the body, but to a body that is more abstract than ever.[1]

Derrida further writes that the spectre is 'what one imagines, what one thinks one sees, and which one projects'.[2] Through retellings of the Wandering Jew's story, this figure again and again becomes a conjuration of a supernatural Other.

---

[1] Derrida, *Specters of Marx*, p. 157.   [2] Derrida, *Specters of Marx*, p. 125.

Building upon Derrida's work, Steven F. Kruger introduces the term 'spectral Jew', noting that, within Christianity, Jewish people have been constructed and imagined as spectres.³ This fantasy construction of the imagined Jewish Other draws upon racist and antisemitic tropes. In order to expunge the historical Jewishness of the Christian messiah, Christ is presented as 'divine and *human*' but not 'divine and a Jewish male', while to emphasise the sacredness of Christians, Jewish identity is represented almost exclusively through the body of the male Jew that is, in the absence of divinity, a polluted Other.⁴

Representations of Jewish Others in fiction such as Shylock and Fagin embody this kind of spectralisation, but the Wandering Jew is the epitome of this ghostly production. Alison Milbank notes that in the eighteenth and nineteenth centuries, the period in which the Gothic novel first emerged and the Gothic mode was developed, a cultural and religious space of separation existed between Protestant and Catholic worlds.⁵ This separation of culture, religion and theology is even more evident in the space between Christian communities and Jewish ones; it is in this gap that ghosts are produced. The Wandering Jew is a ghostly simulacrum: a Christian imagining of what Jewishness is and upon which to project Christianity's fears and anxieties; depicted as a being of flesh and bone but which does not, nor has ever, existed. This spectre forms part of what Carol Margaret Davison calls the antisemitic 'spectropoetics' of British Gothic fiction that 'raised two related spectres – the spectre of Jewish difference and the spectre of Jewish assimilation'.⁶ The Wandering Jew *does* exist, then, but only spectrally. Preserved and conjured throughout history in folklore, oral traditions and Gothic fiction, conjurations of this spectre reflect an attempt to create a distance between the Christian 'I' (the author) and the Jewish Other (the Wandering Jew as subject) that is repeated with each retelling.

The spectral existence of the Wandering Jew is fragmentary. History is replete with versions of him, particularly following his inclusion within Matthew Paris's influential historical work *Chronica Majora* (1259). With each new iteration, new ideas, characteristics and traits are superimposed onto existing versions of the Wandering Jew in texts that at once reconstruct and rework previous versions, interpolating him into new contexts. As Lampert-Weissig notes, Paris's version is foundational but itself draws upon Roger of Wendover's chronicle *Flores Historiarum* (1228) and reproduces the earlier text 'almost verbatim'.⁷ New to Paris's work, however, is an illustration which is one of the first extant depictions of the Wandering Jew.

---

³ Kruger, *The Spectral Jew*, p. 3.   ⁴ Kruger, *The Spectral Jew*, p. 3.
⁵ Milbank, *God and the Gothic*, p. 1.
⁶ Davison, *Anti-Semitism and British Gothic Literature*, p. 7.
⁷ Lampert-Weissig, 'The Transnational Wandering Jew and the Medieval English Nation', p. 774.

Each new version still resembles and bears visible traces of earlier versions (sometimes explicitly), and thus the Wandering Jew's spectral existence is also palimpsestic. Writing in *Blackwood's Magazine* in 1845, Thomas de Quincey turned to the palimpsest. A palimpsest is, he details, a roll of parchment or vellum that has been cleansed of its original manuscript and then a secondary element written upon it, taking the place of the earlier writing. Vellum was costly, and so this process, repeated regularly across generations, saved the cost of creating new writing materials. However, through nineteenth-century scientific advances seemingly magical transformations could occur upon these parchments in which 'traces of each successive handwriting, regularly effaced, as had been imagined, have, in the inverse order, been regularly called back [...] so, by our modern conjurations of science, secrets of ages remote from each other have been exorcised from the accumulated shadows of centuries'.[8] Though the figurative aspect of palimpsests is not new, De Quincey's essay inaugurated the concept of the palimpsest in terms of a 'consistent process of metaphorization'.[9] And a key aspect of this metaphorisation is the ghostly characteristics of the palimpsest. As a palimpsest, the spectre of the Wandering Jew functions like de Quincey's parchment vellum: handed down through generations, the original and subsequent versions of the legend have been erased and new versions superimposed, but traces of earlier renditions can still be recalled and conjured.

Gérard Genette later uses the term 'palimsestuous' to describe reading what he calls the hypertext. The hypertext or palimpsest 'always stands to gain by having its hyper textual status perceived' and often authors will incorporate paratextual clues to encourage such readings.[10] The pleasure of the hypertext and the enduring popularity of, and return to, hypertexts like the Wandering Jew myth is that reader and author enter into a kind of game.[11] Conjuring the ghost of the Wandering Jew invites what Genette calls a 'relational reading', or what Philippe Lejeune has defined as a 'palimpsestuous reading', whereby texts manifesting this ghost are transformed into 'uncanny harbingers' of spectral and palimpsestuous mysteries that invite readers to become detectives.[12] Present-day readers enter into a relationship of detective resurrection where reading a hypertext becomes an act of discovering and resurrecting clues, palimpsestuous connections and the historical significance of former hypertexts. Some connections are harder to decipher than others, but this contributes to the 'thrill of detective discovery'.[13] Sarah Dillon also characterises 'palimpsestuous' as a term that describes the 'type of relationality reified in the

---

[8] de Quincey, 'The Palimpsest', 739–743 (741). [9] Dillon, *The Palimpsest*, p. 1.
[10] Genette, *Palimpsests*, p. 398. [11] Genette, *Palimpsests*, p. 399.
[12] Dillon, *The Palimpsest*, p. 13. [13] Dillon, *The Palimpsest*, pp. 12–3.

palimpsest': as two texts collide with each other through their related layers, the palimpsestic process leads to the 'subsequent reappearance of the underlying script'.[14] So, to give an example using case studies that will later be explored in this Element, a contemporary reader of Sarah Perry's *Melmoth* (2018) may be driven to investigate its relationship with Charles Robert Maturin's *Melmoth the Wanderer* (1820), which might then lead them to discover earlier Wandering Jew hypertexts. Of course, a reader may not actively engage with earlier texts, but they are nonetheless absorbing the varied iterations of a myth that has evolved over many centuries by reading one of the most recent layers written atop the Wandering Jew palimpsest.

As a figurative palimpsest, the Wandering Jew is a double ghost: the spectral conjuration of a Jewish Other that also possesses a palimpsestuous relationship with previous versions which might otherwise seem to have been eradicated. But, in fact, the ghostly traces of these earlier spectres remain to be glimpsed beneath the surface. There is not one ghost of the Wandering Jew, but a genealogy of Wandering Jew ghosts connected through palimpsestuous relationality. The term palimpsestuous, Dillon further argues, draws our attention to '[Michael] Dillon's suggestion, that we must make a word strange in order to enable a renewed and increased intimacy with it. Palimpsestuous relationality, "palimpsestuousness", treads the line of the problematic of incest'.[15] Among the vast and expanding genealogy of Wandering Jew ghosts, there is no one iteration that can claim to be the original wanderer. Rather, each spectre embodies claims of both legitimacy and illegitimacy through their palimpsestuous intimacy with other spectres, and considerations of the Wandering Jew in turn must always consider this figure not as a single spectre but as a family of ghosts.

Beneath the layers of Otherness that construct the spectral Wandering Jew is the Christian self and Christian anxieties. Christian theology posits that Christ will return, and the notion of waiting for this return is not a Jewish experience – as many Jewish people are still awaiting the first appearance of the Messiah or Messiahs – but a Christian one. Similarly, the concept of the Second Coming reflects distinctly Christian concerns that Christ may not return and messianic promises will remain unfulfilled; that Christians will not be redeemed through salvation; and that there will be no 'end' but simply an undetermined period of waiting. These anxieties are entwined with the early Christian belief that this return would occur within the lifetime of Jesus's disciples (see Matt. 24:34; Mark 13:30; and Luke 21:32), and the non-occurrence of this prophesied event subsequently created space for the fear of broken messianic promises.

---

[14] Dillon, *The Palimpsest*, p. 4.   [15] Dillon, *The Palimpsest*, p. 5.

Cursed to traverse the Earth until the Second Coming, the Wandering Jew likewise waits for this return and with it *his* forgiveness, salvation and a cessation to his wandering through death. Christian anxieties are thus projected onto an abstract, spectralised Jewish body that is alienated from the Christian body and self. Often depicted as a Jewish convert to Christianity, the Wandering Jew further reflects anxieties of conversion, but also of Christian Supersessionism; that is, the Christian theological tradition that argues that Christians have superseded Jews as God's chosen people, and that Christ's New Covenant has replaced the former covenant that was exclusive to Jews. Disrupting a Jewish narrative that begins with God's covenant with the Jewish nation, Christianity lays claim to God's covenant and rewrites the Jewish prophesied return to Israel with its own eschatology. The story of Christianity itself thus possesses a palimpsestuous relationship with Judaism, which the Wandering Jew reflects as it represents not simply the construction of an imagined Jewish spectre, but a Christian spectre too.

As the distance between the period in which early Christianity first developed and the present continues to grow, subsequent generations expecting the Second Coming have necessarily contended with the notion that this return has not happened, at least not *yet*. Aslı Iğsız suggests that the concept of the palimpsest is a powerful way to analyse the 'many histories of the present', to explore the possibilities contained within historical ruptures and to reveal the 'process of enfolding' that connects the past to the present.[16] If the emergence of Christianity marks a rupture from Judaism, then the Wandering Jew and the many layers of this myth enfolds this rupture into the present moment and responds to the many histories, but also the many imagined futures, of the present. In parallel with, or perhaps as a consequence of, the continual non-occurrence of the prophesied return, generations of storytellers repeatedly create new versions of the Wandering Jew.

Part of this palimpsestuous enfolding is also located in the reader. When reading a Wandering Jew text, for example, we must accept that we may not be the author's intended audience, or even their contemporaneous readership, and moreover that our interpretations are influenced by our personal experiences and knowledge of different historical contexts. A reader in the present may, like the author, be a Christian waiting for the prophesied End Times, but such a reader would also possess the knowledge that any expected apocalypse did not occur in the author's lifetime. Present-day readers also have an awareness of the violent history of antisemitism in the twentieth and twenty-first centuries, which are often born out of traditions of Christian antisemitism. This includes

---

[16] Iğsız, 'Theorizing Palimpsests', 192–208 (193–4).

the Holocaust, a genocide driven by Nazi ideology that weaponised fictional narratives and popular mediums to promote an antisemitic agenda. Nazi Germany's Minister of Propaganda, Joseph Goebbels, saw German cinema as the 'vanguard of the Nazi troops', and propaganda films like *Der Ewige Jude* (*The Eternal Jew*; 1940) were used to promote the Nazi's antisemitic agenda.[17] Considered with historical hindsight, any Wandering Jew hypertext is therefore palimpsestuously connected to a reader's knowledge of the Holocaust and Nazi propaganda, and as the many histories of the present are enfolded into our understanding of the past, present-day readers of Wandering Jew narratives will necessarily engage with such texts in a different way to their contemporary readership. We can consider this as a double haunting: through the spectral palimpsest of the wanderer, the past continues to haunt the present, but the present also haunts the past.

The Romantic period was a particularly productive moment in the Wandering Jew's history, where the figure as we know him today was fully realised in the Gothic mode. Fundamental aspects of the Gothic novel are 'entrapment by a constricting past' and 'superstitious fears', and these elements are also central to the Wandering Jew myth in which consequences of the past are enfolded into the present moment along with fears regarding possible futures.[18] Notable prose conjurations of the figure in this period include Lewis's *The Monk* (1796), a novel responsible for (re)introducing and popularising the Wandering Jew within Britain, William Godwin's *St. Leon* (1799) and Percy Bysshe Shelley's derivative retelling *St. Irvyne* (1810), and Maturin's *Melmoth the Wanderer* (1820). George Croly's *Salathiel* (1828), though not solely a Gothic novel, employs Gothic techniques and tropes to create a historical and biblical iteration of the myth. Retelling the Wandering Jew's story, each novel constructs distinct versions: Lewis creates a Gothic version who carries a brand that recalls the mark of Cain; Godwin creates an ostensibly secular version connected to forbidden secrets of alchemy; Shelley echoes Godwin's version, but reintroduces an explicitly Christian denouement; Maturin bifurcates the Wandering Jew myth in a story that features both an English/Irish Faustian wanderer and a supernaturally aged Jewish man entombed underground; and, finally, Croly focuses on the Wandering Jew as a biblical eyewitness. These depictions are distinct, but they also contain traces of earlier versions, embodying the palimpsestuous relationality and spectralised nature of the Wandering Jew. Moreover, the narrative trajectory of each conjuration is tied to a period of waiting (for the prophesied end; for death; and for either salvation or damnation), thus revealing the Christian anxieties that lie beneath these tales.

---

[17] Eisner, *The Haunted Screen*, p. 329.   [18] Milbank, *God and the Gothic*, p. 17.

Like other studies of Gothic wanderers and immortals including Marie Mulvey-Roberts's *Gothic Immortals: The Fiction of the Brotherhood of the Rosy Cross* (1990) and Tyler R. Tichelaar's *The Gothic Wanderer: From Transgression to Redemption* (2012), this study will take a chronological approach to uncover the palimpsestuous developments of the spectre of the Wandering Jew in early Gothic fiction. The sections that follow will uncover key genealogies of the Wandering Jew that emerged in the Romantic period and investigate its palimpsestuous relationship with alchemy, Faust and biblical history. The concluding section will turn to Perry's *Melmoth*, exploring this novel as contemporary Wandering Jew hypertext and excavating the palimpsestuous layers through which past iterations are enfolded into the present. However, before turning to these works, the rest of this section will trace the origins of the Wandering Jew and establish the central characteristics of the myth. Beginning with the history and early development of the Wandering Jew, I will then turn to explore Lewis's Gothic wanderer and the early proliferation of the Wandering Jew in the Romantic period.

Origins of the Wandering Jew Myth

Though it is difficult to locate the exact genesis of the Wandering Jew, the version conjured in Matthew Paris's *Chronica Majora* is often considered to be the 'most influential medieval written source of the legend'.[19] Paris was an English Benedictine monk and early historian, and *Chronica Majora* attempts to chronicle world history from biblical Creation up to the year of Paris's death. In an entry titled 'Of the Jew Joseph who is still alive awaiting the last coming of Christ', this work records the story of Cartaphilus (Joseph) as recounted by an Armenian archbishop on pilgrimage to England. Notably, before ending up in Paris's chronicle, this version was diffused through several oral, interpretative and written layers: Paris's entry is a copy of the earlier historical account by Roger of Wendover, while the story itself purports to have been orally conveyed by an Armenian archbishop, and is further filtered through his French interpreter. Through these layers, we discover that Cartaphilus was a porter in the service of Pontius Pilate who physically struck and mocked Jesus:

> [he] said in mockery, 'Go quicker, Jesus, go quicker, why do you loiter?' And Jesus looking back on him with a severe countenance said to him, 'I am going, and you will wait till I return.' And according as our Lord said, this Cartaphilus is still awaiting his return; at the time of our Lord's suffering he was thirty years old, and when he attains the age of a hundred years, he always returns to the same age as he was when our Lord suffered.[20]

---

[19] Lampert-Weissig, 'The Transnational Wandering Jew and the Medieval English Nation', p. 774.
[20] Paris, *Flowers of History*, p. 513.

This entry contains several key features of the Wandering Jew myth: a transgression against God; a curse; prophetical End Times; a supernatural bodily transformation and youthful regeneration; and conversion to Christianity. Although privileging his converted identity, the story nonetheless represents the figure's dual identities and reveals an apparently indissoluble link to his former Jewish identity. However, while later versions build upon this foundation and add new layers (while others trace a different lineage altogether), the Roger/Paris version is itself constructed through pre-existing parts. Noting that the transmission of the legend is multilingual and transnational, Lampert-Weissig identifies a thirteenth-century oral tradition that claims the Wandering Jew was seen in Armenia.[21] Lampert-Weissig also highlights that the myth dates back to the sixth century,[22] while in an 1853 volume of his *Miscellany*, George Reynolds posits that the legend may have originated from the words of Jesus documented in the Gospel of John.[23] In response to an enquiry about John, Jesus replies, 'If I will that he tarry till I come, what *is that* to thee' (John 21:22), and Reynolds states that 'In consequence of this expression we are told, "the saying went abroad among the brethren, that that disciple should *not die*"'.[24] As this concept of an immortal waiting for the return of Jesus spread throughout Europe, it transformed, in part, into the legend of the Wandering Jew.

Within the British tradition of the myth, the Paris text is the most influential in introducing and popularising the figure. There are, however, other notable strands that develop alongside Paris's Cartaphilus and eventually merge together. Eino Railo states that, concurrent to the development of Cartaphilus, figures named Malchus and John Buttadeus – the former taking inspiration from John 18:10 in which Simon Peter strikes the high priest's servant Malchus during Jesus's arrest, and the latter possibly inspired by the Italian word *buttare* which means to strike – emerged and reflected ideas of eternal wandering and punishment.[25] Yet, *The Wandering Jew's Chronicle*, first published in 1634, better epitomises his construction within the British tradition. *The Wandering Jew's Chronicle* is a popular English broadside ballad that recounts the history of English monarchs from William the Conqueror, and was continually reprinted until its final publication in 1830.[26] Demonstrating its popularity, other printed ballads often stated that they should be sung 'To the Tune of

---

[21] Lampert-Weissig, 'The Transnational Wandering Jew and the Medieval English Nation', p. 774.
[22] Lampert-Weissig, 'The Transnational Wandering Jew and the Medieval English Nation', p. 772.
[23] Reynolds, 'The Wandering Jew', 280 (280). [24] Reynolds, 'The Wandering Jew', p. 280.
[25] Railo, *The Haunted Castle*, p. 193.
[26] The first known record of *The Wandering Jew's Chronicle* is an entry in the Stationers' Register to Thomas Lambert in 1634. For a detailed overview of all of the editions of the ballad, see the Bodleian Library's archive wjc.bodleian.ox.ac.uk/index.html.

The Wandering Jew's Chronicle', while, to ensure the ballad's continued relevance and commercial value, subsequent editions 'reprint, continue, interpolate, and amend the core text, resulting in new versions that typically bring the narrative up to date with the present'.[27] It existed in print and oral traditions concurrently, with parts of it taken and added to other works while the core print text was added to and amended with entries on subsequent monarchs and various illustrations also appended to different editions. There is, therefore, no one definitive version of *The Wandering Jew's Chronicle*. Like the figure of the Wandering Jew itself, this ballad can be viewed as a palimpsest, with new versions replacing old versions, though parts of previous versions can still be glimpsed (or heard) in later ones. Though he narrates the ballad, the unnamed Wandering Jew is not an active character in its events, and instead functions as a proverbial witness to England's monarchs while validating a Royalist and Protestant perspective of English history. The ballad therefore conjures the Wandering Jew in order to chronicle not a Jewish experience, but an English, Christian one. In this way, its publication history and the changing nature of the text itself can be viewed as analogous to the mercurial nature of the myth.

We can use the analogy of the production of *The Wandering Jew's Chronicle* to trace the many versions of the Wandering Jew. Beyond the spectral presence of this figure in texts that have him bear witness to the origins of Christianity, he is also constructed using parts taken from the Hebrew Bible and Jewish mythology. Among the many names conferred upon this figure are Ahaseurus and Ahasver, names that appear throughout the Hebrew Bible in the Books of Esther, Ezra and Daniel. Derrida writes that 'Inheritance from the "spirits of the past" consists, as always, in borrowing [...] the borrowing *speaks* borrowed language, borrowed names'; this aspect of appropriation is evident in the spectralised construction of the Wandering Jew.[28] Ahasuerus is the King of Persia, who was not Jewish, and Galit Hasan-Rokem emphasises that this name was an odd and perhaps unsuitable choice for the Wandering Jew as 'its first bearer in the Hebrew Bible was a pagan and his role in postbiblical legend made his name unfit for any Jewish child'.[29] The name Ahasuerus, when given to the Wandering Jew, speaks volumes. It declares an identity that appears on the surface to be Jewish, but whispers beneath its surface that this identity is artificial and borrowed, and that those who assign this name to the Wandering Jew to signify a Jewish identity lack a full understanding of the original biblical

---

[27] Bergel, Howe, and Windram, 'Lines of succession in an English ballad tradition', 540–62 (542, 551).
[28] Derrida, *Specters of Marx*, p. 136.
[29] Hasan-Rokem, 'The Enigma of a Name', 544–50 (545).

figure. Perhaps, then, it is an apt name for a spectralised, imagined figure such as the Wandering Jew.

Another name borrowed from the Hebrew Bible and retroactively associated with the Wandering Jew is Cain, the firstborn son of Adam and Eve introduced in the Book of Genesis and whose story has since been revised, retold and amended in several apocryphal tales.[30] Genesis 4 depicts Cain's murder of his brother Abel, after which Cain is cursed by God for his transgression: 'now art thou cursed from the earth [...] a fugitive and a vagabond shalt thou be in the earth [...] Therefore whosoever slayeth Cain, vengeance shall be taken on him sevenfold. And the Lord set a mark upon Cain, lest any finding him should kill him' (Genesis 4:11–15). If Cain cannot be killed, this raises the idea that he cannot die and has therefore been wandering ever since, and, noting their similarities, E. Isaac-Edersheim suggests that within the Wandering Jew 'further wanders Cain'.[31] The image of the Wandering Jew contained in Paris's *Chronica Majora* demonstrates the palimpsestuous intimacy shared between the Wandering Jew and Cain, as he is shown hunched over and carrying a mattock: a symbol often associated with the biblical figure. And, as the Wandering Jew was conjured into British Gothic literature in *The Monk*, Lewis also exploited this association.

Origins of the Wandering Jew's Gothic Genealogy in *The Monk*

In his review of *The Monk*, Samuel Taylor Coleridge paid particular attention to Lewis's Wandering Jew, praising it for displaying 'a great vigour of fancy' and pronouncing that 'we could not easily recollect a bolder or more happy conception than that of the burning cross on the forehead of the wandering Jew'.[32] Davison characterises this depiction as the Wandering Jew's 'memorable cameo début in British Gothic literature',[33] and Tyler R. Tichelaar further notes that Lewis's novel is 'primarily responsible for the Wandering Jew becoming an important Gothic figure'.[34] Building on previous iterations, Lewis's brief, but influential, portrayal contains clues that reveal palimpsestuous relations to former conjurations. And, if a detective reader is unsure of this figure's identity, then a Cardinal-Duke is helpfully available to provide confirmation that 'He had no doubt of this singular Man's being the celebrated

---

[30] For example, writing about Cain in *The Legends of the Jews*, Louis Ginzberg observes the apocryphal belief that Cain was fathered by Satan (1937, p. 105).
[31] Isaac-Edersheim, 'Ahasver', pp. 195–210 (p. 205).
[32] Coleridge, 'The Blasphemy of The Monk', pp. 39–43 (p. 40).
[33] Davison, *Anti-Semitism and British Gothic Literature*, p. 96.
[34] Tichelaar, *The Gothic Wanderer*, p. 45.

character known universally by the name of "*the wandering Jew*"'.[35] Lewis is not simply resurrecting old Wandering Jew spectres, however, but adding his own layers, too.

Fleshing out his version, Lewis prominently affixes a distinct variant of the mark of Cain to his Wandering Jew in the form of 'a burning Cross impressed upon his brow'.[36] Railo notes that Spanish variants of the Wandering Jew bestowed upon him a mark of God in the shape of a flaming cross,[37] and Lewis's decision to emblazon this symbol on the forehead of his wanderer not only symbolises the figure's initial rejection of Christianity, but also enfolds the history and significance of Cain into that of the Wandering Jew. As Tichelaar states, 'Cain was already understood to be a wandering outcast, while Abel was commonly interpreted as a character similar to Christ; Cain's murder of Abel was compatible with that of the Wandering Jew as an example of how the Jewish people were blamed for murdering Christ.'[38] This connection between the Wandering Jew and Cain is further suggested through other echoes of the Genesis story in the novel, for example in a reference to 'the Almighty's vengeance' and Lewis's characterisation of the Wandering Jew as a 'fugitive'.[39] Building upon hypertexts of the Wandering Jew that insert him into the Passion narrative and which connect him with John 21:22, Lewis makes allusions to the language and themes of the Genesis story and borrows the mark of Cain to create connections between Genesis 4, Cain and the Wandering Jew. Shaping the undefined mark into a burning cross turns Cain's physical brand into a symbol of Christianity, and in branding a figure identified as *Jewish* with a symbol of Christianity Lewis highlights the tension between Christianity and Judaism that is central to the myth. Moreover, the power and horror of the Christian God's vengeance is solidified in this cross as it burns eternally on the forehead of a being punished for transgressing.

Lewis's Wandering Jew is an exorcist. He enters the narrative to conjure the ghost of the Bleeding Nun, and to give Raymond (who is being haunted by her) the tools to exorcise and lay her spirit to rest. Lewis's depiction of his spectralised Wandering Jew reflects, however, a different kind of conjuration. Derrida writes that the conjuration of spectres creates a relentless pursuit that repeatedly convokes the spectre that they try to conjure away 'in order to chase after him, seduce him, reach him': 'One sends him far away, puts distance between them, so as to spend one's life, and for as *long a time* as possible, coming close to him again.'[40] The Wandering Jew is conjured into narratives and then exorcised from them only to be conjured again within another story.

---

[35] Lewis, *The Monk*, p. 172.   [36] Lewis, *The Monk*, p. 172.
[37] Railo, *The Haunted Castle*, p. 193.   [38] Tichelaar, *The Gothic Wanderer*, p. 46.
[39] Lewis, *The Monk*, pp. 176–7.   [40] Derrida, *Specters of Marx*, p. 175.

The revival of the myth in the seventeenth century occurred almost concurrently to the readmission of Jews to England,[41] while the popularity of the Gothic Wandering Jew in British literature developed in parallel to the significant rise in Jewish immigration in the 1790s.[42] In this way, the mythical figure reflects key Christian anxieties surrounding Jewish communities. Unlike the Bleeding Nun, the Wandering Jew, and therefore the Jewish Other, cannot be forgiven or laid to rest because the structure of his myth demands that this only happen as part of Armageddon. Until then, Christian authors can only pursue this figure through their stories, adding their own layers to his construction.

The mark of Cain is one of the key layers that Lewis appends to the Wandering Jew, and his unique depiction subsequently inspired several imitations. Ghasta, the principal wander from Shelley's 1810 poem 'Ghasta; or, The Avenging Demon!!!' for example, entreats the listener to 'Look upon my head' where 'Of glowing flame a cross was there'.[43] Similarly, Paolo from Shelley's *The Wandering Jew* states that 'a burning cross illumed my brow'.[44] The repeated use of this specific mark – a burning cross placed on the brow of the wanderer – invokes again not only the Wandering Jew but specifically Lewis's wanderer, bringing with it the borrowed spectre of Cain via Lewis. Shelley also adds his own layers, linking Paolo's mark to specific aspects of Christian eschatology: 'God's mark is painted on my head; / must there remain until the dead / Hear the last trump, and leave the tomb, / And earth spouts fire from her riven womb.'[45] Later, in *Melmoth the Wanderer*, Maturin too alludes to such a mark as he describes Melmoth wiping a hand over his 'livid brow, and, wiping off some cold drops, thought for the moment he was not the Cain of the moral world, and that the brand was effaced, – at least for a moment'.[46]

Another key feature of Lewis's wanderer is his 'large, black, and sparkling' eyes that inspired 'a secret awe, not to say horror'.[47] His eyes captivated characters within Lewis's novel and his enthralled readers, including Coleridge, and Heidi Thomson suggests that Coleridge's continual interest in the Wandering Jew can be seen in an early reference to a romance he had planned to write ('Wandering Jew, a romance') and *The Wanderings of Cain,* a planned collaboration with William Wordsworth.[48] However, it is in *The Rime of the Ancient Mariner* (1798), and particularly the 'glittering eye' of his Mariner, that the

---

[41] Davison, *Anti-Semitism and British Gothic Literature*, p. 2.
[42] Rubinstein, *A History of the Jews in the English-Speaking World*, p. 6.
[43] Shelley and Shelley, 'Ghasta', pp. 50–62 (pp. 60–1).
[44] Shelley, *The Wandering Jew*, Canto III, line 689.
[45] Shelley, *The Wandering Jew*, Canto III, lines 573–6.
[46] Maturin, *Melmoth the Wanderer*, p. 299.   [47] Lewis, *The Monk*, p. 168.
[48] Thomson, 'Wordsworth's "Song for the Wandering Jew' as a Poem for Coleridge", 37–47 (41–2).

relationship to Lewis wanderer is most evident.[49] Coleridge's Mariner is often viewed as a Wandering Jew figure and can be considered to be a genealogical descendent who also manifests aspects of the Flying Dutchman legend. Hypnotic eyes and mesmeric powers have since become a popular element of Gothic Wanders, and are attributed not just to the Wandering Jew and Coleridge's Mariner but to diverse characters including Melmoth the Wanderer, Dracula and Svengali.[50]

The publication of *The Monk* immediately caused a public outcry. Claims that it was pornographic and blasphemous led to its being debated in Parliament, and Lewis subsequently released a bowdlerised version expunging many of the parts deemed scandalous. However, its legacy, and in particular the legacy of Lewis's Bleeding Nun and Wandering Jew, lived on beyond the novel as a wave of related publications explicitly promoting their relationship to Lewis's novel satiated the public's growing appetite for these stories. Chapbooks (later known as Penny Dreadfuls) were 'cheaply manufactured, sometimes garishly illustrated, and meant to be thrown away after being read to pieces',[51] and consequently many do not survive today. However, some chapbooks have been preserved, including several chapbook versions of Lewis's novel such as the anonymously published *Almagro & Claude; or Monastic Murder; Exemplified in the Dreadful Doom of an Unfortunate Nun* (1810) and Sarah Wilkinson's *The Castle of Lindenberg; or, the History of Raymond and Agnes* (1820), both of which conjure the Wandering Jew.[52] The novella *The Castle of Lindenberg* (1798), also capitalises on the popularity of the Bleeding Nun and the Wandering Jew.[53] Though it is essentially a republished version of the secondary narrative of Raymond and Agnes in *The Monk*, new to *The Castle of Lindenberg* are two illustrations, one of which depicts the exorcism of the Bleeding Nun at the very moment that Lewis's Wandering Jew dramatically reveals his flaming mark. Taking a different direction and transforming Lewis's tale into parody, R. S. Esq.'s *The New Monk* (1798) burlesques Lewis's distinctive Wanderer. Here, Lewis's Raymond figure is replaced with a character named Henry who is haunted by the ghost of the Bleeding Doctor, and the exorcism is performed by an individual known as the man with the tail. Initially identified as Dr Katterfelto to create a caricature of Gustavus Katterfelto, a famous eighteenth-century Prussian conjurer, scientist and quack who often performed

---

[49] Coleridge, 'The Rime of the Ancient Mariner', pp. 5–23, line 3.
[50] Tichelaar, *The Gothic Wanderer*, p. 49.   [51] Frank, *The First Gothics*, p. 433.
[52] For more details about chapbooks see Potter's *Gothic Chapbooks, Bluebooks and Shilling Shockers, 1797–1830*.
[53] The novel's full title is *The Castle of Lindenberg; or, the History of Raymond and Agnes; with the story of the Bleeding Nun; and the Method by which the Wandering Jew Quieted the Nun's Troubled Spirit*.

with a black cat, this individual is later humorously identified as 'the wandering Jew, or one of the wise men of Gotham'.[54] As he performs the exorcism, Dr Katterfelto simultaneously lampoons the Prussian conjurer's black cat and satirises Lewis's mark of Cain.[55]

Despite initially receiving public opprobrium, Lewis's novel and his Wanderer enjoyed both familiarity and popularity as they were continually devoured and adapted in later works. Part of the appeal of texts like *The New Monk*, *The Castle of Lindenberg* and the various chapbook reworkings of *The Monk* is the palimpsestuous intimacy they share with Lewis's novel and his Wandering Jew. *The Monk* is partly responsible for introducing, or *re*-introducing, the Wandering Jew into Britain. Though the Wandering Jew takes up only a small number of pages in *The Monk*, it remains one of the most prominent depictions of this figure in the Romantic period and within the Gothic more broadly. Other notable conjurations include a version of the *Wandering Jew's Chronicle* that was circulating in the 1790s under the title *An Old Song, Newly Reviv'd; Or, The Wandering Jew's Chronicle*, but Lewis's depiction typifies conventional constructions of the figure that would be enfolded into subsequent Gothic versions.

Capitalising on *The Monk*'s enduring popularity, an 1809 edition of *La Belle Assemblée* invokes German legends and literature with reference to Lewis's novel. Here, two German stories are published: the first is a popular German legend titled 'Laurenstein Castle; or, The Ghost of the Nun' (similar to Lewis's Bleeding Nun narrative); the second is a prose translation of Christian Friedrich Daniel Schubart's 'Der ewige Jude. Eine Lyrische Rhapsodie' (1783; 'The Eternal Jew: A Lyrical Rhapsody'). The Wandering Jew/Bleeding Nun episode within *The Monk* occurs in Ratisbon, Germany and, in the novel's advertisement, Lewis credits the tradition of the Bleeding Nun to Germany and the Castle of Lauenstein in North Bavaria. The German legend circulated in *La Belle Assemblée* resembles the Bleeding Nun portion of *The Monk*, although occupying the place of the exorcist in this story is not the Wandering Jew but an old lieutenant. However, the placement of the prose translation of Schubart's poem directly after this legend allows the reader to invoke Lewis's wanderer as they are directly invited to recall *The Monk*: '*Our readers are acquainted with the uses to which Mr Lewis, in his Novel of the Monk, has converted the ancient legend of the Wandering Jew. – The original story was the invention of the celebrated Schubart.*'[56] Here, the editor has performed the role of detective and takes enjoyment in sharing cryptic clues they have uncovered in

---

[54] R. S. Esq., *The New Monk*, vol. 2, p. 68.   [55] R. S. Esq., *The New Monk*, p. 60.
[56] 'The Wandering Jew', *La Belle Assemblée* (February 1809), 19–20 (p. 19). Original emphasis.

Lewis's novel relating to earlier Germanic legends. Earlier in 1801, *The German Museum* also published an English prose translation of Schubart's poem, but the arrangement of the two stories in *La Belle Assemblée,* with the prose translation of Schubart's poem following a translation of the legend of the Ghost of the Nun, consciously mimics the structure of *The Monk*, conjuring first the Bleeding Nun and then the Wandering Jew into its narrative. The reader can therefore glimpse past constructions of the figure as they are enfolded into their present consideration of recent Gothic iterations.

The editor of *La Belle Assemblée* erroneously states that the Wandering Jew is Schubart's invention, yet although his poem is but one iteration within the German tradition, it is nonetheless significant in establishing the Wandering Jew as suicidal:

> Rome, the giant, collapsed into rubble,
> I positioned myself under the collapsing giant,
> Yet it fell without crushing me.
> Nations arose and sank before me;
> But I remained, and did not die!
> From the could-girded cliffs I plunged
> Down into the sea; but swirling waves
> Rolled me to the shore, and the flaming arrow
> Of Being pierced me again.[57]

The futile attempts at suicide made by Schubart's wanderer are emblematic of the figure of the Wandering Jew itself who cannot be killed or exorcised, only continuously conjured, resurrected and pursued. Lewis's novel appeared before the 1801 or 1809 prose translations, but as Lewis was fluent in German he likely read Schubart's poem. Consequently, Lewis resurrects a key feature of the Wandering Jew introduced by Schubart in *The Monk*: the suicidal wanderer. We can, for example, compare Schubart's poem to a similar passage in *The Monk* where Lewis's wanderer proclaims, 'Death eludes me, and flies from my embrace. In vain do I throw myself in the way of danger. I plunge into the Ocean; the Waves throw me back with abhorrence upon the shore: I rush into fire; The flames recoil at my approach.'[58]

Another key feature of Schubart's wanderer is his name, Ahasver. Lewis's Wandering Jew remains nameless, but Ahasver (or variations such as Ahasverus/Ahasuerus) appear in the 1801 and 1809 prose translations as well as subsequent versions that draw on both *The Monk* and Schubart's poem. Borrowed from the

---

[57] Schubart, '"The Eternal Jew: A Lyrical Rhapsody" (1784)', pp. 379–82 (p. 380).
[58] Lewis, *The Monk*, p. 169.

Hebrew Bible, the name Ahasuerus can also be traced to the German tradition and a 1602 pamphlet: *Kurtz Beschreibung und Erzehlung von einem Juden mit Namen Ahasuerus* (*Brief Description and Narration of a Jew Named Ahasuerus*). Observing that in 1602 there appeared at least twenty different editions of the anonymous *Kurtz* pamphlet, R. Edelmann states that it is responsible for making the Wandering Jew 'common property for the broad masses all over Europe and a source of further development within European folklore'.[59] Like other productions of the figure that preceded and followed the publication of *Kurtz*, this pamphlet added new layers to an old story of conversion. Ahasuerus appears prominently in the pamphlet's title, and Tamara Tinker highlights that 'Naming the Wanderer [...] after the Persian king in the Old-Testament Book of Esther who befriends the Jews, arrogates to Christianity a figure celebrated by Jews at Purim and puts a formerly Popish convert in the service of German Protestantism'.[60] In the many versions of *The Wandering Jew's Chronicle*, the Wandering Jew is exploited to endorse a Royalist and Protestant construction of English history and nationalism; similarly, the Wandering Jew is utilised in *Kurtz* to promote a Protestant vision of German nationalism.

The *Kurtz* pamphlet highlights the role played by the Wandering Jew in German legends and popular constructions of German nationality, and revered German writers such as Schubart, Friedrich Schiller and Johann Wolfgang von Goethe later appropriated this figure into Germany's eighteenth- and nineteenth-century literary canon. We can also see the interconnected nature of these national traditions as British writers engaged with these German texts. It is very probable, for example, that Lewis read Schiller's *The Ghost-Seer* in its original German prior to its English translation and was therefore aware of the text's mysterious wanderer figure, the Armenian.[61] Moreover, Lewis was certainly apprised of a version of Goethe's *Faust* in its original German, and Byron confesses in his letters, 'His [Goethe's] *Faust* I never read, for I don't know German'; but Matthew Monk Lewis, in 1816, at Coligny, translated most of it to me viva voce.[62] Of course, taking place in 1816, this incident occurs long after the publication of *The Monk*, and we can only guess as to whether Lewis was acquainted with Goethe's original *Faust: Ein Fragment* (*Faust, a Fragment*) which appeared in 1790, although Syndy M. Conger argues that Lewis may have heard reports of what is known as the *Urfaust*

---

[59] Edelmann, 'Ahasuerus, The Wandering Jew', pp. 1–10 (pp. 5, 8).
[60] Tinker, *The Impiety of Ahasuerus*, p. 1.
[61] Colosimo, 'Schiller and the Gothic – Reception and Reality', pp. 287–301 (p. 290).
[62] Byron, 'Letter 377', vol. 4, pp. 320–1 (p. 320).

manuscript while he was in Germany in 1792.[63] Bryon's anecdote appears in response to Goethe's own praise for Byron's *Manfred*, Goethe having drawn similarities between Byron's Manfred and his own Faust, and while neither Manfred nor Faust are explicitly identified as the Wandering Jew, these characters operate in conversation with his legend. Like many in this period, Goethe was fascinated by the figure. He writes in his autobiography that 'I now took up the strange idea of treating epically the history of the Wandering Jew, which popular books had long since impressed upon my mind',[64] while a letter penned by Goethe in 1786 further reveals his interest in tracing the origins of Christianity through this legend who would have 'been a witness of all this wonderful development and envelopment'.[65] Although Goethe regarded the figure a 'worthy ingredient' for a poem,[66] it is one creative project he evidently started but never finished, turning his attention instead to the Wandering Jew's relation, Faust.

The palimpsestic nature of the spectralised Wandering Jew is exposed with each new retelling that recalls previous versions while concurrently interpolating new elements. The Wandering Jew spectre is therefore not a singular ghost, but rather a family of ghosts. Each spectre is incestuously connected to all of the other Wandering Jew and Wandering Jew-type spectres that precede and follow them, and readers of Wandering Jew hypertexts are implicitly invited to play detective and uncover clues and palimpsestuous relationships that exist between texts. Different national traditions develop unique elements, but they are also deeply interconnected, having influenced each other in a kind of cross-pollination. Thomas Percy's *Reliques of Ancient English Poetry* (1765), for instance, includes an entry on the Wandering Jew that outlines sources from Matthew Paris and the German tradition. Following the publication of *The Monk*, 1797 saw the Wandering Jew take to the stage in Andrew Franklin's comedy *The Wandering Jew; or, Love's Masquerade* (1797). One reviewer writes that this farce will prove 'an universal and lasting favourite of the Public',[67] and although in reality this is not a play about the Wandering Jew, the Wandering Jew myth is central to its romance and comedy. Later, in 1830, the Wandering Jew returned to the stage in a play titled *The Sea Devil; or, The Wandering Jew*.[68] This legend was likewise conjured by the Romantics including Shelley and Coleridge, and also Wordsworth in his 1815 poem 'Song for the

---

[63] See Conger, *Matthew G. Lewis, Charles Robert Maturin and the Germans*, pp. 28, 37. What is now known as *Faust: Part One* was later published in 1808, with *Faust: Part Two* published posthumously in 1832, a year after Goethe completed it.
[64] Goethe, *The Autobiography of Goethe*, p. 35.   [65] Goethe, '*Terni, Oct. 27*, pp. 345–8 (p. 347).
[66] Goethe, *The Autobiography of Goethe*, p. 64.   [67] Anonymous, 'The Theatre', 364–5 (365).
[68] Nicoll, *A History of Early Nineteenth-Century Drama*, vol. 2, p. 522. The author of this play is unknown.

Wandering Jew'. Michael Scrivener argues that the Wandering Jew was 'a mythological construct by which Romantic writers idealized their estrangement from dominant social norms'.[69] Romantic and Gothic wanderers alike were often developed in conversation with the Wandering Jew myth as some authors unequivocally conjure the legendary figure while others took parts of the myth to create figures that can be viewed as related Wandering Jew-type figures. Each conjuration, though unique and distinct, is inextricably connected to previous versions as different traditions, contexts and characteristics are woven together. And, following Lewis's prominent Gothic iteration, Godwin's 1799 novel *St. Leon* soon established a new Gothic trend of Rosicrucian or alchemical wanderers. Turning away from explicitly religious narratives to those of alchemy, but still manifesting palimpsestuous relationships with preceding Wandering Jew hypertexts, this tradition merged proto-scientific advancements with the occult as it created tales of alchemists, sorcerers and necromancers.

2 Alchemical Reproductions: *St. Leon* and *St. Irvyne*

In a letter addressed to Ibrahim Haly Cheik (who is, we are told, a Man of the Law), a strange tale is recounted regarding an individual claiming to be the Wandering Jew. This tale bears traces of previous iterations of the myth and describes a man who claims he was cursed by Christ for insulting him: 'the *Messias* answered him again; *I go, but tarry thou 'till I come*; thereby condemning him to live till the Day of *Judgement*'.[70] This man proclaims that, along with the crucifixion of Christ, he also witnessed the fires that devastated Rome during Nero's reign, the building of Suleiman's ('Solyman') Royal mosque in Constantinople, and the wars in the Holy Lands among many other historically significant events. This man further asserts, in several different languages, that he has travelled to every corner of the globe, and even escaped from the prisons of the Inquisitions. Yet, the veracity of his claims is contested in the opening lines of this letter: 'Here is a Man [...] who pretends to have lived about these sixteen Hundred Years. They call him the *Wandring Jew* [sic]. But some say, he is an *Imposter*.'[71] This letter is one of many that appeared as part of the *Letters Writ by a Turkish Spy* volumes. The first volume was originally published in both French and Italian between 1684 and 1686, with an English translation appearing in 1687. Subsequent editions of these volumes continued to be printed throughout the eighteenth century, and this letter in particular draws on a fascination with not just the Wandering Jew, but notable figures related to him.

---

[69] Scrivener, 'Reading Shelley's Ahasuerus and Jewish Orations', 133–8 (134).
[70] Marana, *The Second Volume of Letters Writ by a Turkish Spy, Who Lived Fiver and Forty Years, Undiscover'd, at Paris*, Book III, Letter 1, p. 181.
[71] Marana, *The Second Volume of Letters Writ by a Turkish Spy*, Book III, Letter 1, p. 180.

This ever-growing family of ghosts related to the Wandering Jew included figures who were, perhaps, Wandering Jew imposters, or possibly other immortal individuals connected to alchemy and black magic. Concurrently emerging in Britain alongside the Wandering Jew, translations of German works such as Friedrich Schiller's *The Ghost Seer* (1787–89) and Karl Friedrich Kahlert's *The Necromancer; or, The Tale of the Black Forest* (first appearing in 1794 under the alias Lawrence Flammenberg) popularised mysterious figures who are alleged to be in possession of secret, magical powers. Like the Wandering Jew, Schiller's Armenian and Kahlert's Necromancer are societal outcasts shrouded in mystery and superstition. They also appear to possess secret, supernatural abilities, yet while the Wandering Jew's longevity and supernatural abilities originate from a curse from God, the source of the occult powers of alchemists, sorcerers or necromancers is more mysterious, potentially linked to science or black magic. Ultimately, however, the supernatural nature of figures like the Armenian and the Necromancer is exposed as counterfeit and the result of fraud and trickery, just as the Wandering Jew from the *Turkish Spy* letters was supposed to be an imposter. In *St. Leon* (1799), William Godwin draws on both the tradition of the Wandering Jew and his associated 'imposters', particularly alchemists; but Godwin's mysterious wanderer *does* in fact possess secret, supernatural knowledge which is then passed on to the eponymous protagonist, who then becomes an alchemical wanderer himself.

Marie Mulvey-Roberts places the Wandering Jew among the 'unhallowed tribe of Gothic immortals', a group that also includes the vampire, Faust, and the alchemist or Rosicrucian sage.[72] If the Wandering Jew belongs to a family of ghosts that are connected through incestuous, palimpsestuous layers, then these other immortals function as close relatives who often weave in and out of Wandering Jew hypertexts and influence the textual lineages of these figures. Shared characteristics include immortality, while other features like a cursed existence, damnation, societal exile, supernatural abilities or scientific expertise manifest in some immortals but not all. Though the alchemist is distinct as a mythical figure in his own right, as Mulvey-Roberts's *Gothic Immortals* (1990) illustrates, the paths of both alchemist and Wandering Jew frequently intersect and many characteristics of the alchemist have subsequently become enfolded into Wandering Jew hypertexts. I want to suggest that we can view alchemical wanderers as a distinct branch of the Wandering Jew's genealogy. Following the popularisation of Rosicrucian adepts skilled in the secret art of alchemy in the Romantic period, Wandering Jew tales

---

[72] Mulvey-Roberts, *Gothic Immortals*, p. 1.

including *Melmoth the Wanderer* (1820) and *Salathiel* (1828) continue to allude to this particular lineage. Godwin's *St. Leon*, which conjures an alchemist who clearly belongs to the pantheon of Wandering Jew figures, is key to this development. Godwin's influence on the evolution of supernatural wanderers is also evident in the work of his future son-in-law Percy Bysshe Shelley, who reproduces and refashions Godwin's tale with an added Faustian twist in *St. Irvyne* (1811).

Godwin's Alchemical Wanderers

Published in 1799, *St. Leon: A Tale of the Sixteenth Century* is Godwin's second novel. This work tells the tale of a French aristocrat and soldier, Count Reginald de St. Leon, who drives himself into madness and leads his family into poverty as a result of his gambling addiction. The Gothic mode is particularly elastic and versatile, allowing for creative development and evolution of a variety of traditions, and in *St. Leon* Godwin merges elements of the myth of the Wandering Jew and the history of Rosicrucian pursuits with 'the Gothic novel and the psychological thriller'.[73] The first volume chronicles St. Leon's military rise and then his societal fall, tracing how his gambling debts force his wife to sell their possessions before the family decide to leave France altogether. Now in Switzerland, the family experience the realities of poverty, natural disaster and the unfair consequences of private ownership which results in the family losing their home. St. Leon also endures a period of insanity. Eventually, however, St. Leon and his family are able to establish a life for themselves on a farm at Lake Constance. But this is not where the story ends. In the second volume, a stranger enters and disrupts the narrative and the life of St. Leon with an offer of a powerful but secret gift: the alchemical secrets of the elixir of life and the ability to transmute metals into gold. Tempted by being the sole living possessor of this secret alchemical knowledge (as receiving this gift would also bring about the stranger's death) and imagining the possibilities of indefinite wealth and eternal life, St. Leon accepts this gift, and in doing so is transformed into a Wandering Jew-type figure who has to live with the consequences of his actions.

On the surface, *St. Leon* is not a traditional Wandering Jew story: there is no reference to the crucifixion; no God or Jesus figure who curses the wanderer; and no anticipation for Armageddon. Godwin was, like his father and grandfather before him, a Dissenting or Nonconformist minister, but after resigning his ministerial post to become a writer, he eventually lost his faith and even embraced atheism. The Wandering Jew story is an obvious influence for

---

[73] Mulvey-Roberts, *Gothic Immortals*, p. 5.

St. Leon, but Godwin turns away from the Christian roots of the myth to create an ostensibly secular version: one tied to alchemy rather than Christ. Yet, beneath the surface, Godwin's narrative still hinges on a rupture caused by a transgressive act – one that violates the perceived natural order of life and death through alchemy – and the aftermath of this act, which leads St. Leon to lead a cursed, immortal existence as a societal outcast like the Wandering Jew.

Alchemy blends the occult with the proto-scientific. A medieval precursor to chemistry, alchemical study and the secret Brotherhood of the Rosy Cross centred around the alchemist's search for the philosopher's stone, immortality and the ability to transmute base matter into gold. However, as Mulvey-Roberts suggests, the origins of the Rosicrucian tradition likely has its roots in the Lutheran Reformation. The possible origin of Rosicrucian pursuits can be traced back to a Lutheran theologian, Johann Valentin Andreae, 'whose family arms bore the symbols of the rose and cross' – connoting 'the dying Christ on the blood-stained cross' – and were later used by Martin Luther himself.[74] Lutheran theology professes that humans are saved from their sins by God's grace alone and that salvation can only be achieved through faith, while Rosicrucian traditions such as those recorded in the *Confessio Fraternitatis* (an anonymous pamphlet published Germany in 1615 and the second of three Rosicrucian manifestos that declared the existence of a secret brotherhood of alchemists) similarly maintain that the secrets of nature can only be discovered through God.[75] What, then, becomes of alchemists who pursue these secrets and transgress the established natural order of human mortality in violation of God?

Godwin's stranger, and then St. Leon himself, are not biblical sinners like the Wandering Jew, but alchemists. However, though *St. Leon* is ostensibly secular, in this novel Godwin creates a hypertext that establishes palimpsestuous connections with both the explicitly religious narrative of the Wandering Jew myth as well as Rosicrucian legends and the Lutheran theology that underpins alchemical narratives. Palimpsests are created by a process of layering which involves erasure and superimposition; yet, while new texts add new layers, they are still haunted by former texts.[76] This is true of Godwin's novel. As Tyler R. Tichelaar acknowledges, though Godwin was probably more influenced by Rosicrucian legends, the Wandering Jew myth is clearly important to the construction of *St. Leon*.[77] The story of the Wandering Jew is a cautionary tale about transgressing against God, and early traditions of Rosicrucian adepts similarly emphasise the importance of unlocking the secrets of alchemy through

---

[74] Mulvey-Roberts, *Gothic Immortals*, pp. 2–3.   [75] Mulvey-Roberts, *Gothic Immortals*, p. 5.
[76] Dillon, *The Palimpsest*, pp. 9, 12.   [77] Tichelaar, *The Gothic Wanderer*, p. 51.

a relationship with God. *St. Leon* is a Gothicised cautionary tale that combines these two traditions.

While the Wandering Jew awaits Christ's return, the alchemical wanderer also contends with the material absence of God. Moreover, early Rosicrucian sages worked as part of a collective brotherhood, their objectives complementing Lutheran principals that knowledge and salvation can only be achieved through God, and echoes of this can be seen in the depiction of the stranger's alchemical secrets: 'The talent he possessed was one upon which the fate of nations and of the human species might be made to depend. God had given it for the best and highest purposes; and the vessel in which it was deposited must be purified from the alloy of human frailty.'[78] *St. Leon* suggests that, like Rosicrucian pursuits, the secrets of alchemy are discovered only through God and by individuals deemed to be worthy of divine secrets. Yet, unlike Rosicrucian brotherhood, the alchemical wanderer of *St. Leon* acts alone in a perpetual state of wandering exile, his possession of secret knowledge an ungodly transgression. Underneath the many layers of Rosicrucian mystery in *St. Leon* is a story of alchemical wanderers that echoes that of the Wandering Jew: Godwin's characters transgress through alchemical pursuits and attain immortality, but they also cursed with exile and a fixation upon their deferred death.

St. Leon reveals Godwin's interest in the paranormal. Though he did not revisit these themes in his fiction, his final publication *Lives of the Necromancers* (1834) returns to this subject, documenting stories of magic and mysticism. In the Preface to *St Leon*, Godwin quotes at length from *Hermippus Redivivus: Or, The Sage's Triumph Over Old Age and the Grave* (1744), a text that chronicles historical and anecdotal examples of alchemy and the pursuit of immortality. Purportedly written by John Campbell, *Hermippus Redividus* is in fact the last and most famous medical satire of German physician Johann Heinrich Cohausen and explores the idea of prolonging life.[79] Despite its satirical nature, *Hermippus Redivivus* documents examples of figures distinguished within alchemical traditions, and it is one of these, Signor Gualdi, that Godwin revives in his Preface. Gualdi arrives in Venice a stranger; he appears knowledgeable in all subjects, pays for everything in ready money and owns a vast collection of paintings. Sparking intrigue in those he meets, Gualdi's identity is challenged when the uncanny resemblance between himself and one of his paintings is observed: 'You look [...] like a man of fifty, and yet I know

---

[78] Godwin, *St. Leon*, pp. 164–5.

[79] For more information about *Hermippus Redivivus* see Anna Marie Roos's 2007 article, 'Johann Heinrich Cohausen (1665–1750), Salt Iatrochemistry, and Theories of Longevity in his Satire, *Hermippus Redivivus* (1742)'.

this picture to be one of the hand of Titian, who has been dead one hundred and thirty years, how is this possible?'[80] Gualdi soon departs Venice, leaving the reality of his identity to speculation. Godwin's conclusion is that Gualdi was in possession of the Philosopher's stone and with it 'the art of transmuting metals into gold, and the *elixir vitae*'.[81] *Hermippus Redivivus* is one of many texts that recount similar stories of mysterious individuals appearing in cities such as Venice, Hamburg and Paris and who are linked to alchemy, longevity and the Wandering Jew himself, including the potentially fraudulent encounter recorded in *Letters Writ by a Turkish Spy*. Godwin views alchemy with scepticism, and concludes his Preface by acknowledging the impossibility of such tales. But, clearly they fascinated him.

In *St. Leon*, Godwin conjures not one but two Wandering Jew-type figures or alchemical wanderers, merging the transgression and social exile of the Wandering Jew with Rosicrucian legends. First, in the middle of the narrative and at a time when St. Leon has finally found contentment, a stranger enters the novel. His outward appearance conforms to the typical representation of the Wandering Jew as old and ostensibly poor: 'He was feeble, emaciated, and pale, his forehead full of wrinkles, and his hair and beard as white as snow. [...] His garb, which externally consisted of nothing more than a robe of russet brown, with a girdle of the same, was coarse, threadbare, and ragged. He supported his tottering steps with a staff.'[82] Though this mysterious stranger appears poor and wretched, St. Leon immediately perceives 'traces in his countenance' that suggests he is 'no common beggar', and it is this perception that encourages St. Leon to offer his assistance.[83] The stranger is not what he seems: echoing the story of Gualdi, Godwin's stranger initially introduces himself to St. Leon as a Venetian called Francesco Zampieri, but his name and nationality are eventually revealed to be fraudulent. While his exterior projects old age and poverty, he reveals that he possesses inestimable wealth and the secrets of eternal life. As Carol Margaret Davison argues, the name 'Zampieri' suggests a kind of anti-semitic exoticism, and there are further hints within the narrative that this figure is the actual Wandering Jew, or has, perhaps, traded his soul to the original Wandering Jew in return for the secrets of alchemy (a deal he now offers to St. Leon).[84] He is no ordinary beggar, and his construction clearly bears traces of both the Wandering Jew and legendary alchemists.

Unlike the traditional Wandering Jew, however, the stranger is able to die – but not before passing on his secrets (and his curse) to St. Leon. While the mystery surrounding the stranger's identity reveals the influence of both the

---

[80] Godwin, 'Preface', in *St. Leon* pp. 50–2 (p. 50). [81] Godwin, 'Preface' in *St. Leon*, p. 51.
[82] Godwin, *St. Leon*, p. 155. [83] Godwin, *St. Leon,* p. 155.
[84] Davison, *Anti-Semitism and British Gothic Literature*, p. 107.

Gualdi legend and the Wandering Jew myth, Marie Mulvey-Roberts posits that Godwin may also have been influenced by the story of reputed alchemist Nicholas Flamel.[85] Godwin's protagonist is descended from a line of distinguished French counts, and notably the French town of Leon is central to the story of Flamel as the place of his alchemical discovery.[86] Flamel was a fourteenth-century French scribe, but after his death the belief that he was in fact an alchemist in possession of the philosopher's stone flourished, a belief undoubtedly bolstered by an alchemical work *Livre des figures hiéroglyphiques* (*The Book of Hieroglyphic Figures*, 1612) posthumously ascribed to Flamel and his supposed possession of a manuscript thought to be a Kabbalistic text titled *The Book of Abraham the Jew*.[87] Believing the manuscript to have been 'stolen or taken from the miserable Jews', and unable to decipher its strange language and enigmatic pictures, Flamel turns to the Jewish community for help.[88] In the town of Leon, Flamel eventually discovers a physician: a Jewish convert to Christianity. This individual successfully interprets the mysteries of the book before passing on these secrets to Flamel.[89] Flamel's story thus connects Jewish Kabbalistic traditions with Rosicrucian traditions. Like crypts, palimpsestic hypertexts contain hidden information that can be resurrected by attentive readers. Such information can be hidden through 'cryptic incorporation' or encryption, whereby ghosts of former texts live on spectrally through the palimpsest, ready to be resurrected through palimpsestuous reading.[90] Although not cited by Godwin in his Preface, the next episode recounted in *Hermippus Redivivus* after the story of Gualdi is that of Flamel, suggesting that Godwin was aware of this story. Whether or not Godwin intended to make these associations, a palimpsestuous reading connects his wanderer with the Flamel legend, and with it both Rosicrucianism and Kabbalah.

But while Godwin's novel is built upon many earlier tales, it also adds new layers to the Wandering Jew palimpsest. For example, Godwin introduces the idea of cursed individuals who bequeath their secrets and their curses to new wanderers, adding a cyclical aspect to the Wandering Jew story. This allows for the central tenets of the myth – connected to ideas of damnation and salvation, deferred death and redemption from transgression – to be severed from a need to

---

[85] Mulvey-Roberts, *Gothic Immortals*, p. 51

[86] Another possible source inspiring the name 'Leon' is Moses de Leon, a thirteenth-century Spanish rabbi and Kabbalist who was for many years believed to have been the sole author of the *Zohar*, one of the central and most widely read Kabbalistic books. See Horowitz, *A Kabbalah and Jewish Mysticism Reader*, p. 103.

[87] An English translation of this work first appeared in London in 1624 under the title *Exposition of the Hieroglyphical Figures*.

[88] Flammel, *Alchemical Hieroglyphics*, p. 9.   [89] Flammel, *Alchemical Hieroglyphics*, p. 18.

[90] Dillon, *The Palimpsest*, pp. 6, 29.

wait for Christ's return. While the traditional Wandering Jew must await prophesied events beyond his control, here the alchemical wanderer can pass on this mantle by convincing another to transgress. However, the cycle of repetition created by this ability to pass on knowledge, and thus suffering, emphasises key elements of the Wandering Jew's story. Following the disruption caused by the stranger, St. Leon's story replicates the structure of the traditional myth, where transgression is followed by punishment and the wanderer's eventual exile from society. Assuming the mantle of the alchemical wanderer, St. Leon puts his knowledge of alchemy into practice, hoping to bring about good both for his family and wider society. However, his alchemical gifts only create misery. First, his family experiences an expulsion from paradise as St. Leon decides they should leave their home at Lake Constance and re-enter French society. Subsequently, his newfound wealth is viewed with suspicion because he cannot account for it. His son chooses estrangement from his father and his corrupted wealth, stating that 'I shall not be contaminated with an atom of it'.[91] His servant and dog are both killed. His wife dies in childbirth, having delivered a stillborn baby. The lives of his daughters are tainted, ending in ruin or death. And St. Leon himself is forced to reckon with his immortal existence alone, as his predecessor did.

In a chain of repetition and cyclical conjuration, St. Leon's transgression and the consequences that follow are depicted as a re-enactment of what the stranger has already experienced. St. Leon's first use of alchemy to regenerate his body to youth recalls the initial moment of rupture caused by the stranger's entrance into the novel. Having escaped imprisonment from the Spanish Inquisition, St. Leon examines himself in a mirror but his reflection is unrecognisable because the person staring back is an eighty-year-old man with hair 'white as snow, and my face ploughed with a thousand furrows'.[92] St. Leon appraises himself as he had earlier assessed the stranger, drawing attention to greying hair and a wrinkled forehead and noting a disjunction between his old appearance and his real age of fifty-four. Rather than looking at himself, then, this passage suggests that St. Leon is once again encountering the stranger, or that their identities have somehow become intertwined as the mirror reflects his predecessor. We can infer that the stranger also endured such a metamorphosis. The bodily transformations involved in becoming an alchemical wanderer recall Paris's Cartaphilus, who repeatedly returns to the age of thirty when he reaches one hundred years old. Since thirty is the age at which Cartaphilus supposedly witnessed the crucifixion, his regeneration underscores his act of transgression. Though the metamorphoses of the stranger and St. Leon must be brought about

---

[91] Godwin, *St. Leon*, p. 213. [92] Godwin, *St. Leon*, p. 341.

deliberately through alchemy, their regeneration similarly serves as an act of remembrance that emphasises the reason for their transformation: their possession and use of secret alchemical knowledge unsanctioned by God.

Further repetitions occur throughout the novel to establish a connection between the stranger and St. Leon, as he experiences things the stranger has already endured: 'I was only acting over again what he had experienced before me.'[93] This includes being pursued by the Inquisition, familial estrangement and losing ties to his country and even his own name. Though the stranger's own act of transgression is withheld from the narrative, we can imagine that St. Leon's act repeats it. To that end, while St. Leon states the condition of his possession of alchemical secrets is 'that they must never be imparted', the possibility remains that he, like the stranger before him, may choose to die and bequeath his gifts to another individual, beginning the cycle anew.[94]

Godwin leaves his alchemical wanderer friendless and without family, but he nonetheless decides not to pass on his secrets and thus his curse. This means that, like the Wandering Jew, he will remain immortal, the possibility of his death projected into an uncertain future. And, also in kind with the Wandering Jew, versions of Godwin's alchemical wanderers live on, conjured in other texts that continue to add new palimpsestic layers to *St. Leon*. Any reader seeking the 'thrill of detective discovery'[95] can not only uncover and resurrect the Wandering Jew through Godwin's novel, but also trace the development of his own wanderer in later hypertexts. A year after the publication of *St. Leon*, Edward DuBois published *St. Godwin* (1800), a satire of Godwin's novel that depicted Godwin himself as the alchemical wanderer, while Godwin's friend John Hobart Caunter later penned *St. Leon: A Drama. In Three Acts* (1835), a play inspired by the novel. Most pertinent to this discussion, though, is *St. Irvyne; or, The Rosicrucian*, by Godwin's future son-in-law Percy Bysshe Shelley. In this novella, Shelley conjures his own alchemist, Ginotti, who tempts Wolfstein de St. Irvyne in order to pass on his alchemical secrets. But Shelley's work does not present itself as secular; instead, it reinstates the explicitly Christian themes common to the Wandering Jew myth, emphasising the role of God in the wanderer's journey – and the Devil, too.

Shelley's Christian Alchemist

Shelley was no stranger to the Wandering Jew. From his early juvenilia such as 'Ghasta; or, The Avenging Demon!!!' (1810) and *The Wandering Jew* (written in 1810 but not published until 1877) to his later poem *Queen Mab* (1813) and

---

[93] Godwin, *St. Leon*. p. 335.   [94] Godwin, *St. Leon*, p. 53.
[95] Dillon, *The Palimpsest*, pp. 12–3.

verse drama *Hellas* (published posthumously in 1822), Shelley continually conjured this figure. Yet, though fascinated with the myth, each figure Shelley manifests is different as he assembles parts borrowed from established versions while adding his own elements. Shelley's varied use of names for the Wandering Jew illustrates how his constructions of this figure evolved throughout his literary career. His earlier poems give the Wandering Jew the names Ghasta' ('Ghasta') or Paulo (*The Wandering Jew*), while later in both *Queen Mab* and *Hellas* he bears the name Ahasuerus. Though they share similarities and connections with previous Wandering Jew hypertexts, each iteration is distinct. This is true even of Shelley's versions that bear the name Ahasuerus; in *Queen Mab* he is a phantom conjured by the Fairy Queen, while in *Hellas* he is a hermit healer. In this way, Shelley's wanderers epitomise the acts of borrowing, revision and 'cryptic incorporation' that are at the heart of the Wandering Jew tradition.[96]

Shelley's interest in the Wandering Jew can be traced back to his fascination with the Gothic and his early literary experimentation. Inspired by Lewis, Shelley gives some of his Wandering Jew figures a Cain-like mark, while he borrowed the name Ahasuerus from elsewhere, probably the prose translation of Schubart's 'Der Ewige Jude' which was published in the *German Museum*. Shelley's cousin Thomas Medwin claims in his own rendition of the Wandering Jew, *Ahasuerus, The Wanderer: A Dramatic Legend* (1823) – a play published a year after Shelley's death – that he shared with Shelley a fragment containing a translation of a German poem about the Wandering Jew.[97] Medwin's play shares particular similarities with Shelley's *The Wandering Jew*, which Medwin claimed to have co-authored.[98] However, this assertion was later challenged by Betram Dobell, who states that Medwin 'was a most inaccurate and misleading writer' and provides evidence for Shelley's sole authorship of the poem.[99]

Though Shelley frequently conjured the Wandering Jew, *St. Irvyne* is his only work that features an alchemical wanderer. Shelley borrows heavily from Godwin's *St. Leon* and these texts share many similarities, not least their titles (taken from the names of their central protagonists, both of which are derived from geographical locations).[100] Mulvey-Roberts considers a commercial basis for these similarities, suggesting that Shelley hoped to 'capitalise upon the success of his predecessor'.[101] Shelley's prose romances are regarded by many as immature juvenilia that are 'unworthy of serious consideration', and consequently, along with *Zastrozzi* (1810), *St. Irvyne* is often omitted from

---

[96] Dillon, *The Palimpsest*, p. 29.   [97] Medwin, 'Preface', pp. vii–xiii (p. viii).
[98] Medwin, *The Life of Percy Bysshe Shelley*, vol. 1, pp. 53–5.
[99] Dobell, 'Introduction', pp. xiii–xxxii (p. xiv).
[100] Mulvey-Roberts, *Gothic Immortals*, p. 67.   [101] Mulvey-Roberts, *Gothic Immortals*, p. 67.

discussions of Shelley's corpus.[102] More recently, however, Stephen C. Behrendt, Kim Wheatley and Mulvey-Roberts have challenged this assumption, critically examining Shelley's prose romances and underscoring the importance of these texts in foreshadowing themes and characters now regarded as emblematic within his oeuvre.[103] Shelley's alchemical wanderer is unique within his Wandering Jew conjurations, but it reflects the tradition's palimpsestic and fragmentary nature, along with Shelley's appreciation for Godwin's works and the Gothic. Paralleling Godwin's novel, the narrative of *St. Irvyne* focuses on the relationship between St. Irvyne and a mysterious bandit initially identified as Ginotti. Just as in *St. Leon*, this stranger tempts St. Irvyne with the secrets of alchemy in order to pass on his cursed existence. However, while Godwin's mysterious stranger passes on the mantle of alchemical wanderer to St. Leon, Shelley rewrites the acquisition of alchemical secrets as a Faustian pact.

Shelley retains key elements of the tradition of alchemy. Hoping to pass on his alchemical gifts, Ginotti bequeaths St. Irvyne a book containing secret instructions, and directs him to take '— and – and —; mix them according to the directions which this book will communicate to you'.[104] Substituted with dashes, the omission of identifiable ingredients evokes the idea of secret knowledge, whilst the unnamed book further encrypts the traditions of alchemy or Kabbalah, recalling the story of Flamel and *The Book of Abraham the Jew*. We do not know how this book came into Ginotti's possession, but we do eventually discover that alchemy is only part of the story. The narrative concludes with Ginotti failing to pass on his curse, as Satan appears and kills both the bandit and St. Irvyne; however, it appears that only Ginotti is damned to a 'hopeless eternity of horror' in Hell.[105] Ginotti implores St. Irvyne to 'deny thy Creator', and St. Irvyne responds, 'Never [...] any thing but that'.[106] Though his temptation to possess the secrets of alchemy leads to his death, St. Irvyne's unwavering Christian faith saves his soul. Emphasising this Christian message, the final lines of *St. Irvyne* contain an appeal to the reader to hope for future salvation beyond death:

> Let then the memory of these victims to hell and malice live in the remembrance of those who can pity the wanderings of error; let remorse and repentance expiate the offences which arise from the decision of the passions, and let endless life be sought from Him who alone can give an eternity of happiness.[107]

---

[102] Behrendt, 'Introduction', pp. 9–53 (p. 12).
[103] See: Behrendt, 'Introduction', pp. 9–53 and Kim Wheatley's 2016 article '"Strange Forms": Percy Bysshe Shelley's *Wandering Jew* and *St. Irvyne*'.
[104] Shelley 'St. Irvyne', pp. 159–252 (p. 238).   [105] Shelley, 'St. Irvyne', p. 252.
[106] Shelley, 'St. Irvyne', p. 252.   [107] Shelley, 'St. Irvyne', p. 252.

Here, a rebuke is placed on those who seek eternal life not through Christianity, but through occult means – be it through a satanic pact or alchemy – and the novel concludes with an affirmation of Christianity and the messianic promise. While there may be many similarities shared between *St. Leon* and *St. Irvyne*, Shelley's version adds an explicitly Christian conclusion, unequivocally presenting the pursuit of forbidden knowledge and possession of alchemical secrets as a transgression against God. This overtly Christian narrative is, perhaps, a strange addition to an ostensibly secular story of alchemy, particularly as Shelley shared Godwin's atheism. However, *St. Irvyne* anticipates later Wandering Jew conjurations such as Charles Maturin's *Melmoth the Wanderer* (1820), a novel that continues to frame alchemical secrets as forbidden knowledge and that also culminates with the presumption that Maturin's eponymous wanderer has been dragged to Hell as a result of his own Faustian pact. Reflecting his own Christianity, and borrowing from *St. Leon* and *St. Irvyne*, Maturin conjures his own Wandering Jew story to warn against ungodly transgressions.

3 Faustian Incarnations: *Melmoth the Wanderer*

At the heart of the Wandering Jew story is an act of transgression against God and rejection of the Christian Messiah. It also holds up a mirror to sacrificial theology or the idea of substitutionary atonement. If the story of Christ is one of sacrificial substitution, whereby the death and resurrection of Christ acts as the ultimate redemptive sacrifice for all of humanity's sin since the original sin committed by Adam and Eve, then the Wandering Jew's rejection of this sacrifice through his mockery of Christ leaves him still indebted to God. The price of this debt is his curse of immortality; he is awaiting not just his death, but atonement and reconciliation with God. Sacrifice and debt are also central to the legend of Faust. In an inversion of the contract between humanity and God, Faust enters into a deal with the Devil and, in exchange for material gain on earth, sacrifices his spiritual immortality in Heaven.

This legend emerged from historical accounts of Johann Georg Faust, a German magician who was sometimes depicted as an alchemist, a physician, a philosopher, an astrologer or simply a fraud. Folk tales about Faust spread across Germany detailing how the Church denounced him for being in league with the Devil, and suggesting his alleged death was the result of an explosion caused by his diabolical alchemical experimentation. Versions of this legend soon circulated across Europe, and eventually it was immortalised in literature. Christopher Marlow's 1592 play *The Tragical History of the Life and Death of Doctor Faustus* brought the legend to a British audience, and later Johann

Wolfgang von Goethe's *Faust* (first appearing as *Faust: Ein Fragment* in 1790, then published in two parts in 1808 and 1832) further popularised the tale in the Romantic period. Key to Marlowe's play is the hope of atonement, and a Good Angel affirms that it is 'Never too late, if Faustus will repent'.[108] At the play's conclusion, Faustus has not repented or accepted God, and so he is eternally damned. This is not the case for Goethe's Faust, who, in *Faust, Part Two*, is successful in his pursuit of salvation: 'Delivered is this noble member Of the spirit world from evil: / He who ever striving takes pains, Him we can save.'[109]

Faust is damned by the Devil while the Wandering Jew is cursed by God, but both are doomed to an immortal existence as they await their fate. Redemption through God is also central to their potential salvation. While the Wandering Jew's prolonged existence is itself a way for him to atone for his transgressions, atonement is possible for Faust at any point before his eternal damnation should he actively seek it. Like the alchemist, the Faustian sinner belongs to the Wandering Jew's family of ghosts, sharing with him characteristics such as immortality, transgression and damnation, spiritual debt and an anxiety surrounding death and the afterlife. Through these shared characteristics we can see the palimpsestuous layers of the Wandering Jew myth as well as the incestuous connections that bind together these figures with the alchemist and other Wandering Jew relatives. In his Gothic novel *Melmoth the Wanderer* (1820), Irish Protestant clergyman Charles Robert Maturin builds on these established and interconnected traditions by weaving together the legends of Faust and the Wandering Jew to create his own Faustian wanderer. The eponymous Melmoth is a Wandering Jew type figure who has sold his sold to the Devil, and has, as we learn through the novel's several narrative layers, spent his immortal life attempting to tempt someone else to take his place and fulfil the his debt of damnation.

The Enemy of Mankind

Ordained into the Church of Ireland in 1803, Maturin became curate of St Peter's Church, Dublin in 1805 and remained there until his death in 1824. But, alongside his religious career, he also pursued a literary one. Like many clergymen in this period, Maturin published collections of his sermons – *Sermons* (1819) and *Five Sermons on the Errors of the Roman Catholic Church* (1824) – alongside seven novels and four plays. Following the success of his first play *Bertram* (1816) published under the pseudonym Dennis Jasper Murphy, he revealed his true identity. Despite *Bertram*'s success, critics such as

---

[108] Marlowe, *Doctor Faustus*, Act 2, scene 2, line 80.   [109] Goethe, *Faust*, p. 419.

Samuel Taylor Coleridge castigated the play as being 'melancholy proof of the depravation of the public mind'.[110] Following such public criticism, the Church of Ireland barred Maturin from any further clerical progression. Though never relinquishing his Dublin curacy, this decision possibly served to embolden Maturin in his literary pursuits, and in particular his enthralment with the popular Gothic genre, while his theological beliefs permeated many of his fictional works, including *Melmoth*.

Melmoth is Maturin's fifth novel. Discussing its publication in a letter to his publisher, Archibald Constable, he frankly confessed his motivation for pursuing a career in literature: 'I write for bread – for the maintenance of my family.'[111] Sharon Ragaz suggests another motivation – literary ambition[112] – to which I would add a third: Protestant evangelism. The result is a Gothic novel that alludes to the Wandering Jew myth and is composed, as a critic from the *Edinburgh Review* writes, using a 'Golgotha style of writing'.[113] Suffering through the many, often confusing narrative layers of Maturin's novel, this critic further laments having to read a multitude of passages 'of similar sound and fury, signifying nothing'.[114] At the heart of the novel, however, is the Wandering Jew. Conjuring a familiar spectre that is, like its typically Christian authors, awaiting Armageddon, Maturin adds his own layers that are rooted in his Protestant faith.

Maturin's dual roles as clergyman and Gothic novelist should not be considered in isolation. As his religious beliefs influenced his fictional works, so too his published sermons reveal his dramatic preaching style and fixation on biblical narratives and themes that would not be out of place in Gothic stories.[115] Tracing the inspiration for *Melmoth*, Maturin states:

> The hint of this Romance (or Tale) was taken from a passage in one of my Sermons [...] The passage is this.
>
> 'At this moment is there one of us present [...] who would, at this moment, accept all that man could bestow, or earth afford, to resign the hope of his salvation? – No, there is not one – not such a fool on earth, were the enemy of mankind to traverse it with the offer!'[116]

---

[110] Coleridge, *Biographia Literaria*, vol. 1, ch. 23.
[111] 'Letter from Charles Maturin to Archibold Constable', undated. Quoted in Ragaz, 'Maturin, Archibald Constable, and the Publication of *Melmoth the Wanderer*', 359–73 (360).
[112] Ragaz, 'Maturin, Archibald Constable, and the Publication of Melmoth the Wanderer', pp. 359–73 (360).
[113] Anonymous, 'Review of *Melmoth, the Wanderer*', 353–62 (359).
[114] Review of *Melmoth, The Wanderer*, *The Edinburgh Review*, p. 357.
[115] See, for example, Sermon, 'On the Death of Lord Nelson' *Sermons* (1819), pp. 49–50.
[116] Maturin, 'Preface', pp. 5–6 (p. 5).

Melmoth thereby functions, as Dale Kramer observes, as a 'sermon in fiction'.[117] Terry Eagleton further notes that *Melmoth* 'stands at the source of the powerful current of Irish fiction known as Protestant Gothic,' suggesting that Maturin's work is permeated not just by a sense of Irish nationalism, but a distinctly Protestant perspective.[118] But, what exactly is it that Maturin is preaching in *Melmoth*?

By 1820, the Wandering Jew was a popular figure and an established trope of Gothic tales since *The Monk*. Contributing to this tradition facilitated Maturin's commercial needs and literary ambitions through the familiarity of this figure, emphasised by the prominence of the word 'Wanderer' in the novel's title, while also complementing his own Protestant theology. Like the Wandering Jew myth, Maturin's sermons drew upon Christian eschatology and contemporaneous anxieties regarding waiting for the End Times, damnation as a consequence of transgression against God and hope for future salvation. The end of any given century typically creates millenarian and apocalyptic trends relating to the prophesied Second Coming and the End Times and, as I will discuss in the next section, this was the case in the 1790s. However, though Armageddon failed to manifest in the year 1800, throughout the nineteenth century theological discussions and conjurations of the Wandering Jew continued to return to these themes, reconsidering and revising eschatological understandings in light of Christian disappointment that the anticipated apocalypse had not yet occurred.

Raising the spectre of the 'enemy of mankind', *Melmoth* focuses on transgression rather than salvation. Drawing, in part, on the Faust legend, the story of Maturin's Wandering Jew figure depicts Melmoth's search for a substitute before the end of a predetermined period of 150 years or he will forfeit his own salvation. As Alison Milbank notes, substitution sacrifice is central to *Melmoth*, and the singular pursuit of its immortal protagonist is to tempt another to take on his burden, acceptance of which 'entails closing the redemptive openness of the possibility of salvation for a reward of rescue from physical harm or insoluble. Sin and guilt are to be exchanged, and the sufferer will become Melmoth's scapegoat.'[119] The initial price of Melmoth's transgression is his own damnation and, as he fails to tempt another into an exchange of this debt, he is dragged to Hell at the novel's conclusion. Underpinning *Melmoth* are themes central to both the Wandering Jew myth and contemporaneous Christian anxieties, but it also reflects a 'Golgotha' style of theology that is infused with dark, gloomy and Gothic fears. Published in the wake of unfulfilled apocalyptic prophecies of the end of the eighteenth century and lacking any hope of

---
[117] Dale Kramer, quoted in Marie Mulvey-Roberts, *Gothic Immortals*, p. 131.
[118] Eagleton, *Heathcliff and the Great Hunger*, p. 187.
[119] Milbank, *God and the Gothic*, p. 201.

salvation, this is a cautionary tale of transgression, damnation and a melancholy period of waiting.

'We live in awful times', Maturin proclaims in a sermon published a year before *Melmoth*: 'it is certainly awful to look around us, and see what *has been*, and feel *what is*, and think what *may be*.'[120] Here, Maturin shares a belief that he lived during a period of waiting for the End, one defined by a hope (or fear) of an imagined future and the transgressions of the past and present. There is little wonder that he found inspiration in the Wandering Jew as a vehicle through which to metaphorically express those anxieties; Melmoth's story hinges on a transgression that curses him to a (limited) period of immortality that will culminate in his death and damnation. Through the novel's palimpsestuous layers, we can glimpse the story of the Wandering Jew who must suffer indefinitely until Christ returns. This suffering is central to Maturin's theology and to *Melmoth*; as Keith M. C. O'Sullivan notes, *Melmoth* is a novel less concerned with the potential for salvation than it is with the 'ordeal of the journey' to deliverance.[121] Where the Wandering Jew's transgressive act marks him as a Christ killer and echoes the act of original sin, Melmoth's transgression is linked to his un-Christian search for secret, forbidden knowledge that is attained not through Christ but by infernal means.

Instead of turning to God, Melmoth seeks out the Devil, travelling across Europe to 'study of that art which is held in just abomination by all "who name the name of Christ"'.[122] His travelling companions include a clergyman as well as Dr John Dee and Albert Alasco. Later, this clergyman is the only witness to Melmoth's staged death. He reports that he listened to Melmoth's 'dying' words, in which Melmoth describes his search as 'the great angelic sin' and 'the first mortal sin – a boundless aspiration after forbidden knowledge'.[123] This turn to alchemy and 'Rosicrucian heresy', Mulvey-Roberts writes, 'may be viewed as a second Fall of mankind'.[124] Melmoth's other companions, Dr Dee and Albert Alasco, are notable for being historical figures associated with alchemy, and both are featured in William Godwin's later *Lives of the Necromancers*. Maturin thus incorporates several elements established by previous manifestations of the Wandering Jew spectre, particularly *St. Leon* and *St. Irvyne*. Melmoth's sinful, Faustian search is associated with alchemy, while the discovery of a portrait of Melmoth by his descendant John Melmoth further recalls Godwin and the traditions of alchemy through the portrait trope.[125] Echoing parts of the story of Gualdi quoted in the Preface of *St. Leon,* the

---

[120] Maturin, '[Sermon] Preached on the Fast-Day', p. 288.
[121] O'Sullivan, 'His Dark Ingredients', 74–85 (81).   [122] Maturin, *Melmoth*, p. 498.
[123] Maturin, *Melmoth*, p. 499.   [124] Mulvey-Roberts, *Gothic Immortals*, p. 8.
[125] Both Melmoth the Wanderer and his descendant are called John Melmoth. To avoid confusion, I will refer to the eponymous wanderer as Melmoth, and his descendant as John.

portrait of Melmoth bears the date 1646 and was therefore painted 150 years before John meets him, exposing Melmoth's supernatural longevity.[126]

This, then, is a Wandering Jew hypertext. Where Godwin's novel merges the traditions of Rosicrucianism and the Wandering Jew, Maturin's *Melmoth*, like Percy Bysshe Shelley's *St. Irvyne*, also weaves in Faustian elements. The hypertext 'always stands to gain by having its hyper textual status perceived', and, as Gérard Genette further notes, authors often go to great lengths to leave clues within their hypertexts and encourage detective discovery.[127] To understand the mysterious Melmoth, readers are invited to uncover the character's inspirations and enter into relational readings with a number of previous wanderers. Like all conjurations of the Wandering Jew, however, Maturin refashions established elements and adds his own layers rooted in his religious beliefs. Whether Melmoth's immortality is owed to alchemy or a deal with the Devil (or both) is not confirmed, but what is important is that his alchemical pursuit of 'forbidden knowledge' is positioned in opposition to the Church and therefore to God: an abomination that even Melmoth himself compares to the transgressions of Satan and original sin.

Just as in the Wandering Jew story, the horror at the heart of Maturin's novel is Melmoth's transgressive act (here his pursuit of forbidden knowledge rather than forsaking Christ himself). In order to further align him with the Wandering Jew, Maturin pairs him – in a novel filled with Gothic doubles – with a Jewish character, Adonijah, a scholar living alone beneath the city of Madrid. Adonijah, perhaps an immortal himself, is the character who reveals the dark secrets of Melmoth's unnatural longevity to Alonzo Monçada, a Spanish monk recently escaped from the Inquisition. We learn that Adonijah had also pursued forbidden knowledge; while Melmoth seeks the secrets of alchemy in Europe, Adonijah pursued Jewish secrets of Egyptian sorcerers. Recounting his life to Monçada, Adonijah confides that:

> In the days of my childhood, a rumour reached mine ears, even mine, of a being sent abroad on the earth to tempt Jew and Nazrene, and even the disciples of Mohammed, whose name is accursed in the mouth of our nation, with offers of deliverance at their utmost need and extremity [...] Like our fathers in the wilderness, I despised angel's food, and lusted after forbidden meats, even the meats of the Egyptian sorcerers. And my presumption was rebuked as thou seest: childless, wifeless, friendless, at the last period of an existence prolonged beyond the bounds of nature, am I now left.[128]

---

[126] The trope of a portrait revealing the supernatural existence of an individual is later picked up by Maturin's great nephew Oscar Wilde in his novel *The Picture of Dorian Gray* (1890). Wilde also took inspiration from his uncle's book as he assumed the name 'Sebastian Melmoth' following his release from Reading Gaol.

[127] Genette, *Palimpsests*, p. 398.   [128] Maturin, *Melmoth*, p. 269.

Adonijah's path is different from Melmoth's – in that the 'secrets' he has sought relate to the magic used by Jewish and Egyptian sorcerers in the Hebrew Bible (Ex. 7) – but yet eerily similar too; in parallel to Melmoth's pursuit of 'forbidden knowledge', Adonijah covets 'forbidden meats'. The repetition of the word 'forbidden' emphasises a shared aspect of their pursuits: both are framed as transgressive acts, and both require unnatural punishment. If the elixir vitae of alchemy is considered to be the Devil's property, then so too the forbidden meats of Egyptian and Jewish sorcery are aligned with the demonic.[129] As Melmoth turns to alchemy and the Devil, Adonijah embraces other traditions of sorcery. In a further parallel, the exact details of their pursuits are shrouded in mystery and unrecorded within the novel thus underscoring the potential dangers of possessing such knowledge. The doubling of Melmoth and Adonijah therefore emphasises the danger of such transgressions against God: there are many ways to be tempted to sin, and Maturin's novel preaches against all of them.

Melmoth and Adonijah are further aligned with the Wandering Jew through their role as chroniclers of history. The Wandering Jew serves as an eyewitness to the origins of Christianity, but also to historical events that support the developing narratives of the faith; for example, in *The Wandering Jew's Chronicle*, the mythical figure is used to communicate a specifically Royalist and Protestant perspective on English history. In *Melmoth*, Maturin engages with the 'storyteller' trope common to the Wandering Jew myth through his doubled wanderers, who together attest to the truth of the author's warning (or sermon in fiction). The novel comprises a series of interconnected narratives, and within this complex structure, Adonijah chronicles Melmoth's transgressions as he shares them with Monçada. In turn, Monçada relates to John that in a previous meeting with Melmoth, the wanderer 'constantly alluded to events and personages beyond his *possible memory* [...] with the fidelity of an eyewitness'.[130] Melmoth's anecdotes refer to the Restoration and other historical events that reveal his unnaturally prolonged life and, importantly, they are told to Monçada as part of Melmoth's endeavours to tempt him. Melmoth presents Monçada with the opportunity to acquire a kind of immortality, while obfuscating that to do so he will need to sell his soul, live a life of misery and face damnation in the afterlife. However, that Melmoth's stories distort the truth is revealed by the countless stories told about *him*. As Adonijah chronicles Melmoth's life, he reveals the wanderer's hidden self and their corresponding transgressions. Adonijah's secrets – both his own and Melmoth's – are disclosed

---

[129] Mulvey-Roberts, *Gothic Immortals*, p. 15.   [130] Maturin, *Melmoth*, p. 228.

to Monçada, John and thus the reader of the novel, until we are convinced that both of their unnaturally long lives were obtained through ungodly means.

Another link between Melmoth, Adonijah and the Wandering Jew is forged by a concentration on the many people they have lost throughout their lifetimes: loved ones who have long since died while they continue to live. This is emphasised by four skeletons that Adonijah keeps in his underground vault. Monçada relates to John that he saw these skeletons himself: two were, in life, Adonijah's wife and child, leaving him cut off from his family through their deaths. That he is surrounded by the skeletons of his family evokes Schubart's 'Der Ewige Jude' where the Wandering Jew carries several skulls up to Mount Carmel, identifying them as his family. In Schubart's poem, the Wandering Jew throws the skulls down the mountain in frustration that he is unable to join his loved ones in the afterlife. Adonijah, though, keeps the bones of his wife and child as reminders of his transgression against God – and, moreover, two further skeletons that relate to Melmoth's transgressions. These skeletons are the remains of people whom Melmoth once tried (and failed) to tempt into taking on his curse. The stories of these individuals – as recorded by Adonijah, translated by Monçada and eventually narrated to John – allow them to testify beyond their deaths to the acts of transgression carried out by Melmoth. Furthermore, these records and relics of the dead highlight that liberation through death and salvation is denied to Adonijah and Melmoth, as it has so far always been denied to the Wandering Jew.

We can also see an echo of the Wandering Jew story in the novel's conclusion, particularly through the fates of Melmoth and Adonijah. Maturin concludes *Melmoth* by relating the demise of his central wanderer, revealing the consequences of Melmoth's failure to find a substitute. After a violent storm, John and Monçada search a precipice surrounding Melmoth's ancestral home in Ireland for evidence of the wanderer's death, discovering 'a kind of tract as if a person had dragged, or been dragged, his way through it [...] something hung as floating to the blast. [John] Melmoth clambered down and caught it. It was the handkerchief which the Wanderer had worn about his neck the preceding night – that was the last trace of the Wanderer!'[131] Melmoth vanishes from the novel, but his death is not tied to the prophesied End Times, and thus the spectre of the Wandering Jew lives on, while Maturin and the reader remain in the awful period of waiting. This ambiguous ending further engenders the 'silent and unutterable horror'[132] of what *may be*, and implicitly recalls the warning of his earlier sermon. The reader is left to presume that Melmoth has been dragged to Hell, and thus Maturin exploits the threat, horror and fear of an imagined

---

[131] Maturin, *Melmoth*, p. 542.   [132] Maturin, *Melmoth*, p. 542.

eternity of damnation. The lesson of Maturin's sermon in fiction is to seek salvation through Christ and to hope for salvation, even in dark times. Salvation may be denied to Melmoth, but Maturin's reader may yet be saved.

While Melmoth is damned in death, Adonijah is denied redemption due to his unnaturally prolonged life. Adonijah's death is never confirmed or even alluded to in the novel – and so it ends with the possibility that he is still alive and entombed beneath Madrid. Living subterraneously, he reveals to Monçada that 'Within this apartment I have passed the term of sixty years', stating further that he rarely ascends to the top of the house 'save on occasions like this, or peradventure to pray'.[133] While Melmoth wanders in and out of all of the novel's narrative layers, Adonijah, at the age of 107, is introduced midway through the novel. Adonijah is periodically invoked in the narratives that follow, but these moments always recall the reader back to his static existence. As Monçada recounts several tales to John, the reader is aware that he originally read and transcribed these stories in 'the vault of Adonijah the Jew'.[134] In contrast to Melmoth, whose identity, story and voice are fragmented across many narrative layers, Adonijah remains fixed to a place and time, his life seemingly unending.

So, we can see a complete depiction of the Wandering Jew in this novel through Melmoth and Adonijah as Maturin effectively bifurcates the mythical figure into two characters: Melmoth is a wanderer but not Jewish; Adonijah is Jewish but not a wanderer. Melmoth's status as a 'wanderer' is repeated throughout the text: as well as the novel's title, he is identified as 'Melmoth the Wanderer' six times throughout the novel, and he further embodies this appellation as he is depicted wandering across the globe and through the book's narrative layers searching for someone to take his place. In contrast, Adonijah is a Jew living in a secret subterraneous vault and who appears to be, like Melmoth, in possession of a form of immortality as a consequence of his transgression.

Yet, unlike Melmoth, Adonijah does not seek a scapegoat to take his place, and he enlists Monçada only to assist in his record-keeping. Literally entombed, Adonijah 'the Jew'[135] instead appears suspended in a moment of living death. '[W]hen my task is completed,' Adonijah states, 'then will I be gathered to my fathers, trusting surely in the Hope of Israel, that mine eyes shall "behold the King in his beauty, – they shall see the land that is very far off"'.[136] Quoting Isaiah 33:17, here Adonijah expresses his own distinctly Jewish beliefs regarding a future state of bliss, where Jews will be redeemed by God and reunite with

---

[133] Maturin, *Melmoth*, pp. 265, 267. [134] Maturin, *Melmoth*, p. 356.
[135] Maturin, *Melmoth*, p. 356. [136] Maturin, *Melmoth*, p. 268.

their family in the afterlife. Ostensibly, this imagined future state appears similar to that hoped for by Christians: the final reward of the righteous is redemption and an eternal state of bliss. It also constructs the physical land of Israel as being fundamental to the creation of a heaven on earth. However, within a Christian framework, Adonijah's Jewishness prevents his seeking salvation through sacrificial substitution. On one hand, to seek a substitute to take his place would still leave him damned – or at the very least denied salvation in Heaven – simply because he is Jewish. On the other, accepting the sacrificial atonement offered through Christ would necessitate a rejection of his Jewish identity and conversion to Christianity. Exemplifying Derrida's notion of the production and relentless pursuit of spectres that are repeatedly conjured in order to be pursued and kept close at hand, Jewish spectres like the Wandering Jew denote an alienated past that will, according to Christian theology, eventually be superseded with the prophesied End Times.[137] This prophecy entails the return of Christ along with the conversion of the Jewish people to Christianity in order to bring about a future heaven on earth. However, the Christian period of waiting for this future state has not yet concluded, and thus the spectre of Judaism must remain, like Adonijah, in a state of living death. At the novel's conclusion, hoped-for salvation is denied, or at least deferred; Melmoth is damned, while Adonijah's death remains unconfirmed.

As Maturin adds new layers to the Wandering Jew myth, his two Wandering Jew figures come to represent different but intertwined anxieties tied to the theological foundations of the legend, relating to both the uncertainty of damnation or salvation after death and the as yet unrealised End Times. If we read *Melmoth* as a sermon in fiction, Maturin's doubling of the Wandering Jew reflects a Christian perspective, where the current period of waiting is tied to an acceptance of the Christian Messiah and waiting for an imagined future state. In order to avoid damnation, Maturin's reader must accept Christ, reject offers of forbidden knowledge from the enemy of mankind and refuse to transgress against God. The pursuit of forbidden occult knowledge through alchemy, Faustian deals or through Jewish sorcery will result in damnation – whether in Hell or on Earth.

Whether the lesson of Maturin's sermon in fiction is convincing or not is another question altogether, and evidently the reviewer for the *Edinburgh Review* was not convinced, writing that *Melmoth* presents 'such a burlesque upon tragic horrors, that a sense of the ludicrous irresistibly predominates over the terrific; and, to avoid disgust, our feelings gladly take refuge in contemptuous laughter".[138] French novelist Honoré de Balzac, however, thought

---

[137] Derrida, *Specters of Marx*, p. 175.
[138] Anonymous, 'Review of *Melmoth, the Wanderer*', 353–62 (361).

differently. Balzac considered *Melmoth* to be one of the 'supreme allegorical figures of modern European literature' alongside Molière's Don Juan, Byron's Manfred and Goethe's Faust,[139] and he even penned his own sequel to Maturin's novel, *Melmoth Réconcilié* or *Melmoth Reconciled* (1835). Here, Balzac reimagines the ending of *Melmoth* as his Faustian wanderer does not die, but instead successfully passes on his curse to a dishonest French banker, Castanier. Transforming Maturin's theological lesson from one of damnation and horror into one of hope and salvation, Melmoth finds redemption through repentance:

> Do you know what joy there is in heaven over a sinner that repents? [...] However great the measures of his sins may have been, his repentance has filled the abyss to overflowing. The hand of God was visibly stretched out above him, for he was completely changed, there was such heavenly beauty in his face.[140]

To be saved from eternal perdition, it seems that all you need to do is to repent. And, as Melmoth and then Castanier demonstrate in *Melmoth Reconciled*, if you have been unlucky enough to have been tempted into a Faustian bargain, you need only find someone else to take your place – and there are, it appears, plenty of willing substitutes in modern capitalist society. In fact, Balzac's story descends into absurdity as the Devil's bond is continually exchanged, until the secret power of the Devil is lost to mankind. *Reconciled* is thus a critique of rapacious capitalism as represented by the French stock exchange and a theological lesson on the importance of repentance.

Maturin himself had intended to write a sequel to *Melmoth the Wanderer*, which may have answered some of the novel's lingering questions.[141] It was never written, however, and so the fate of Maturin's wanderer remains ambiguous. This ambiguity is tied to the theological idea of substitutionary atonement found in the earlier Faust narratives of Marlowe and Goethe. Maturin himself preached that 'The "fool, who saith in his heart there is no God," is wise compared to him who saith there is a God, but I will neither acknowledge his justice, nor implore his mercy, nor deprecate his wrath, not ask his forgiveness'.[142] Perhaps, then, Melmoth is twice the fool: he not only transgresses against God in his pursuit of alchemy and a Faustian deal with the Devil, but in seeking a substitute for his sin. Rather than accepting Christ, who, in Christian theology, has already made the ultimate sacrifice to atone for the sins of humankind, he squanders his opportunity to be forgiven and find the salvation that is attained by both Goethe's Faust and Balzac's Melmoth. In any case, Maturin's Faustian novel is built on the

---

[139] Lovecraft, *Supernatural Horror in Literature*, p. 32. [140] de Balzac, *Melmoth Reconciled*.
[141] Tichelaar, *The Gothic Wanderer*, p. 53.
[142] Maturin, '[Sermon] Preached on the Fast-Day', pp. 295–296.

foundations of the Wandering Jew myth, and directly aims to exploit its potential to impart an evangelical message. This potential is later picked up by Reverend George Croly in his novel *Salathiel* (1828), who turns away from Faust and instead returns the myth to its imagined biblical origins.

4 Theological Transformations: *Salathiel*

The 1790s saw an acceleration of Christian millenarianism, with many in Britain anticipating the End Times. Considering the Revolutions in America and France 'unparalleled in the history of nations', Reverend James Bicheno presented his interpretation of scriptural prophecy in *Signs of the Times* (1793): 'clearly do I seem to discern that the last days spoken of by God's servants the prophets, are fast approaching.'[143] Bicheno was a Baptist minister who authored many political-religious publications, and he explicitly roots *Signs of the Times* in his own theology. The title page of this work cites Matthew 24:44 ('Be ye ready; for in such an hour as ye think not the son of man cometh'), but it also references the literary exchange between Joseph Priestly and David Levi. Between 1786 and 1789, Priestly (renowned scientist, philosopher and theologian) and Levi (Anglo-Jewish immigrant and distinguished Hebraist) exchanged a series of public letters discussing Jewish conversion to Christianity. This interfaith debate unfolded in the public arena and inspired several responses, including Bicheno's own *A Friendly Address to the Jews* (1795).[144] Linking his discussion of the imminent End Times to these debates, Bicheno's *Signs of the Times* is emblematic of millennial publications that place anxieties surrounding Jewish identity, nationhood and conversion at the centre of scriptural discourse.

However, when the year 1800 came and went, Christian theologians and Conversionist groups – together with the wider public – had to reconsider when Armageddon might commence. Bicheno, for example, revisited this subject in *A Supplement to the Signs of the Times* (1807). The discourse of prophecy was constantly 'evolving and responding to contemporary events',[145] and although the turn of the century necessitated revised expectations regarding the prophetical End Times, Jewish people and Israel remained central to early nineteenth-century millenarianism. In particular, Supersessionism or Restoration Theology – a Christian doctrine dating back to the third century that asserts that the New Covenant created by Jesus supersedes or replaces the Old Covenant with Jewish people – formed a core tenet of Christianity. Also fundamental to these theological discussions

---

[143] Bicheno, *Signs of the Times*, pp. 4, 5.
[144] Scult, *Millennial Expectations and Jewish Liberties*, p. 80.
[145] Crome, *Christian Zionism and English National Identity, 1600–1850*, p. 203.

is the prophesied return of Jews to Israel along with the conversion of Jews to Christianity. It is against this backdrop that Reverend George Croly published his Wandering Jew tale *Salathiel* (1828). This work engages with contemporary discourse regarding Christian eschatology, Jewish conversion and the physical land of Israel, as well as theological anxieties at the heart of millenarianism and the Wandering Jew myth itself.

A Story of the Past, the Present and the Future

Beginning his career as an Anglican clergyman in Ireland, Croly moved to London in 1810 to pursue his literary ambitions and soon contributed to the *Literary Gazette,* the *New Times* and *Blackwood's Magazine*.[146] Croly's career mirrors that of fellow Irish clergyman and author Charles Maturin; he turned his pen to novels, poetry and plays while also writing hymns and theological works. Following his death in 1860, one biographer wrote that Croly's 'theological works belong to an important order', further declaring that 'His picture of the Wandering Jew in "Salathiel" is one of the most striking efforts ever seen in that class of literature'.[147] This view is shared by contemporary reviewers including *La Belle Assemblée* which praised Croly's depiction of the Wandering Jew and the fall of the Temple, declaring *Salathiel* to be a 'work of infinitely higher order' that '*must* be read'.[148]

Much of Croly's work is critically overlooked due to its overtly evangelical nature, and, like Maturin's *Melmoth,* Croly's millenarianism cannot be divorced from his iteration of the Wandering Jew. However, it is this relationship between popular fiction and Christian evangelism that makes *Salathiel* essential to a study of the Wandering Jew in this period. *Salathiel* follows Croly's poem 'The Restoration of Israel' (1826) and his theological exposition of the Book of Revelation, *The Apocalypse of St John* (1827): central to each text is Israel, the Jewish diaspora and possible future Restoration. *Salathiel* and *The Apocalypse,* in particular, combine End Times narratives with Supersessionism. In contrast to Croly's poetry and religious publications, though, *Salathiel* merges the theological with the supernatural. The novel does not fit neatly into any one genre, blending elements from the Gothic Romance, historical novel and biblical narratives. Yet, while *Salathiel* is not a traditional Gothic novel, the Gothic mode is key to the novel's depiction of Israel and the Wandering Jew, both of which are Gothicised through their continual association with death and ruins,

---

[146] Stephen, *Dictionary of National Biography*, vol. 13, p. 135.
[147] Anonymous, 'The Rev. George Croly, LL.D.', 104–7 (p. 106).
[148] Anonymous, 'The Rev. George Croly, A.M.', 2–10 (pp. 4, 7).

supernatural horror, the haunting of the present by the past and imagined apocalyptic futures.

For Croly, the scriptural End Times was inevitable and imminent. Although framing his interpretation as provisional, Croly believed that Christian prophecy would be fulfilled 'in the year 1863'.[149] The oncoming apocalypse was, for Croly and other millenarians, very real and eagerly awaited. Croly ascribes this expectation to the belief that Christians had succeeded Jews to become God's chosen people. Consequently, possessing the New Covenant, some Christians maintained they now had spiritual claims to the physical land of Israel, a view Croly represents in *The Apocalypse*:

> The mention of Israel does not necessarily imply the Jews. The Christians, the successors of those to whom the promises were given, are called the 'Israel of God,' even to the exclusion of the Jews. The Christians are possessed in the New Testament of the forfeited appellatives that originally belonged to the Jews alone – 'the holy nation;' 'the chosen people;' 'the temple of the living God'.[150]

Croly's version of the Wandering Jew similarly establishes a Christian narrative that hinges on this theological succession. As Steven Kruger notes, the imagined Jew became a spectral presence within Christianity, and although the moment of crucifixion created a new, Christian dispensation, this moment needed to be read backwards as a fulfilment of Jewish, or 'Old Testament' prophecy.[151] Using the Wandering Jew legend, *Salathiel* explores these theological perspectives by returning the reader to this moment of theological transformation, promoting Croly's theology through the Gothic mode. *Salathiel* thus functions, like *Melmoth*, as a sermon in fiction: in exploiting the well-established figure of the Wandering Jew, Croly preaches his perspective of Supersessionism.

Croly roots his fictional story in theology and history, affirming in his Preface that 'this narrative has the supreme merit of truth'.[152] Emphasising his claim to historical and theological accuracy, Croly exploits the trope of the Wandering Jew as an eyewitness to the origins of Christianity, adding new theological layers to the myth. Croly distinguishes his manifestation from previous conjurations stating that 'A number of histories have been invented for him; some purely fictitious, others founded on ill-understood records',[153] and in doing so rewrites the history of the Wandering Jew by claiming previous iterations are

---

[149] George Croly, *The Apocalypse of St John: Or Prophecy of the Rise, Progress, and Fall of the Church of Rome; the Inquisition; the Revolution of France; the Universal War; and the Final Triumph of Christianity. Being a New Interpretation* (London: C. & J. Rivington, 1827), p. 435.
[150] Croly, *The Apocalypse of St John*, p. 97.   [151] Kruger, *The Spectral Jew*, p. xiii.
[152] Croly, 'Preface', pp. v–vii (p. viii).   [153] Croly, 'Preface', vol. 1, p. vi.

fictional while his wanderer is the only true version. The novel further declares that the 'exile lives' and that 'In his final retreat he has collected these memorials'.[154] In this way, Croly reveals the Gothic and palimpsestuous construction of his spectre. As Jerrold E. Hogle asserts, the Gothic embodies an 'insistent artificiality' that often not only includes elements that are 'fake and counterfeit', but 'populates the actual tale with specters of what is *already artificial*'.[155] Horace Walpole's *The Castle of Otranto* (1764) is generally considered to be the first Gothic novel, but the original tale purported to be a genuine translation of a sixteenth century Italian manuscript written by 'Onuphrio Muralto' and translated by 'William Marshal'. Similarly, *Salathiel* also claims to be a genuine found manuscript consisting of 'collected memorials'. However, both Walpole's 'Italian manuscript' (apparently rediscovered in the library of 'an ancient Catholic family')[156] and the 'memorials' that constitute Croly's novel are fictional. Through paratextual material, each text draws on older narratives belonging to an imagined past: *Otranto* is rooted in antiquated Catholic superstition, while *Salathiel* borrows from the Jewish origins of Christianity, both of which Protestant traditions claim to have superseded.

Croly's Preface thus blurs the distinction between historical fact and fiction, and between biblical narratives and legend, serving as an extension of the novel's fictional reimagining of both the Wandering Jew myth and Christian theology. Yet, drawing attention to the fictitious nature of previous Wandering Jew ghosts exposes, perhaps unintentionally, the artificiality of this current iteration. As with all Wandering Jew hypertexts, Croly's Preface explicitly invites the reader to engage in the thrill of detective discovery as they read the following volumes purportedly recounted by the legendary figure himself. The playful mode of hypertextuality, Gennette argues, entails 'some kind of game',[157] and readers are encouraged to uncover relational readings that connect this Wandering Jew with previous versions, while also noting Croly's additions.

The Gothic is a 'deliberate hybrid of the ancient and the modern, of history and fiction', and this deliberate hybridity is true of *Salathiel* too, though Christian narratives are foregrounded.[158] Salathiel cannot die, for example, and in a moment that echoes Schubart's suicidal wanderer, he writes that 'I longed to die [...] I toiled for death; but I remained without a wound'.[159] The final pages of the novel are also devoted to a summation of Salathiel's life up to the present day and briefly chronicles conventional occupations of the wanderer and significant historical events he witnessed. Salathiel, for instance, recounts

---

[154] Croly, 'Preface', vol. 1, pp. vi–vii.   [155] Hogle, 'Introduction', pp. 1–20 (p. 15).
[156] Walpole, 'Preface to the First Edition', pp. 5–8 (p. 5).   [157] Genette, *Palimpsests,* p. 399.
[158] Sage, *The Gothic Novel*, p. 9.   [159] Croly, *Salathiel*, vol. 3, p. 412.

his time spent with Petrarch in Italy and his visit to Germany to pay homage to Martin Luther, while also, in a revelation that recalls Godwin and Rosicrucian study, stating that 'I toiled with the alchemist'.[160] The majority of the novel, however, focuses primarily on the decades between the crucifixion and the fall of the Temple, and Croly's unique retelling thus draws particular attention to the connection between the wanderer and the central tenets of Christianity. Choosing to focus on the figure's origins emphasises its established conventions, bringing to the fore Christian perspectives and anxieties surrounding the wanderer's transgression, the ensuing Christian period of waiting and the anticipated apocalypse that are always integral to Wandering Jew retellings. However, this choice also encourages the reader to further engage in a game of detective discovery in relation to these religious elements. Along with uncovering connections between this Wandering Jew story and those that precede it, the hypertextuality of *Salathiel* relates Croly's wanderer with biblical narratives and contemporaneous historical accounts. This is essentially a retelling of the Gospel accounts as well as Jewish and Early Christian history that employs familiar elements of popular Romantic and Gothic fiction, and in doing so brings the Gospel narratives into conversation with the Gothic mode.

Like the heroes and anti-heroes of Romantic and Gothic fiction who typically possessed 'greater sensibilities' and were 'moral outcasts and wanderers',[161] Salathiel's spectralised perspective reveals him to be increasingly isolated, alienated and melancholy. As he is caught in the divide between his established Jewish community and the emerging Christian one, he wrestles internally with the guilt of his transgression against God and his narrative frequently turns introspective: 'Imagination was to be my tyrant; and every occurrence of life, every aspect of human being, every variety of nature, day and night, sunshine and storm, made a portion of its fearful empire'.[162] Though the novel is as much focused on Salathiel's actions (and their consequences) as it is his repentant introspective thoughts, his increasing alienation and isolation engender sympathy from the reader while the severity of his transgressions are emphasised. At the novel's conclusion he remains isolated not just from his Jewish past, but from the Christian present of the reader too.

The landscape in which Salathiel's story takes place is, furthermore, the familiar but Gothicised landscape of the Bible. Early Gothic novels were often set in European locations – such as Spain and Italy – that British and Irish readers would be familiar with but would unlikely have visited. The same is true of *Salathiel*; even fewer readers would have set foot in Judea or

---

[160] Croly, *Salathiel*, vol. 3, p. 415.   [161] Thorslev Jr., *The Byronic Hero*, p. 18.
[162] Croly, *Salathiel*, vol. 1, pp. 161.

Jerusalem, though knowledge of the Bible would render them familiar. Wandering through Jerusalem, Salathiel remarks:

> I had followed the course of the Kenron, which, from a brook under the walls of Jerusalem, swells to a river on its descent to the Dead Sea. – The blood of the sacrifices from the conduits of the altars curdled on its surface, and stained the sands purple. – It looked like a wounded vein from the mighty heart above. I still stayed on, wrapt in sad forebodings of the hour when its stains might be of more than sacrifice; until I found myself on the edge of the lake. Who has ever seen that black expanse without a shudder? [...] The distant rushing of the River Jordan, as it forced its current through the heavy waters, or the sigh of the wind through the reeds, alone broke the silence of this mighty grave.[163]

This is the Jerusalem of the Bible, but filled with violent and barbaric imagery that evokes visceral reactions in the living while the dead lay 'entombed in sulphurous beds' in the rivers below.[164] Drawing on the Gothic mode, *Salathiel* is brimming with sublime natural prospects, including Mount Carmel that 'towered proudly eminent',[165] awe-inspiring religious buildings and the foreboding scenery of death and the macabre 'tinged by its sepulchral atmosphere'.[166] In one moment, the Wandering Jew is even joined by 'spirits of the evil dead' that have haunted Judea for centuries, one of whom shows Salathiel a vision of the future where the ruins of Judea are 'but the beginnings of evil'.[167]

Here, in a Gothicised Judea, the religious is entwined with the supernatural. Though the traditional Gothic castle or Catholic edifice is absent, in its place is the Holy Temple:

> I see [...] the crowning splendour of all, the central TEMPLE, the place of the SANCTUARY, and of the Holy of Holies, covered with plates of gold, its roof planted with lofty spear-heads of gold, the most precious marbles and metals every where flashing back the day.[168]

As Alison Milbank observes, early Gothic novels are brimming with ruins, and particularly those monastic buildings in which a pleasure is taken regarding the 'fallen ruination of monkish superstition'.[169] While ruined monasteries in actuality speak not to Catholicism but to 'Reformation Britain',[170] in *Salathiel* we see ruination in reverse: narrated by the Wandering Jew, we are told of the grandeur of the Temple of Jerusalem while simultaneously possessing the knowledge of the Temple's later destruction. In other words, we

---

[163] Croly, *Salathiel*, vol. 1, pp. 93–4.   [164] Croly, *Salathiel*, vol. 1, p. 94.
[165] Croly, *Salathiel*, vol. 1, p. 272.   [166] Croly, *Salathiel*, vol. 1, p. 94.
[167] Croly, *Salathiel*, vol. 1, pp. 99, 107.   [168] Croly, *Salathiel*, vol. 1, pp. 26–7.
[169] Milbank, *God and the Gothic*, p. 16.   [170] Milbank, *God and the Gothic*, p. 16.

are aligned with the Wandering Jew, looking back through his memories to the pinnacle of the Holy Temple, but understanding that in our present moment this holy place stands in ruins. Milbank further writes that 'Protestants could look to the toppled towers of abbeys as symbols of the victory over idolatry, so that, paradoxically, the ruins spoke also to them'.[171] This process of appropriation is also true of Jewish narratives and religious places like the Temple of Jerusalem; once exclusively possessed by Jews, such places have been re-sacralised through Christian reinterpretations. Existing spectrally outside of time, Salathiel facilitates this appropriation through ruination as he forges palimpsestic connections between Christianity's Jewish past and its supersessionist present.

And just as Christianity later came to redefine and claim ownership of Jewish religious sites, the conjuration of Judaism through the Wandering Jew is similarly designed to reconfigure Jewishness through a Christian lens. The Wandering Jew is a Christian creation and specifically a spectralised imagined Jew who is made to represent the collective Jewish community from a Christian perspective. Like Maturin's Adonijah, Salathiel continually professes his Jewish identity, stating, for example, 'Israelite as I was, and am'.[172] He is also a Jewish priest, military leader and part of Jewish royalty, and these lived experiences are woven into the novel as Salathiel participates in and commemorates Jewish rituals and customs, observes Passover and the Jubilee year and performs priestly duties. In fact, of all the Wandering Jew figures discussed in this Element, Salathiel is perhaps the one who is most strongly identified with the active and continued practice of his Jewish faith even after the supposedly transgressive act that dooms him.

Croly's wanderer is Salathiel, Prince of Naphtali, and unlike Ahasuerus or Cartaphilus – names which are distinctly not Jewish – the name of Croly's wanderer invokes individuals from the Hebrew bible who *are* Jewish. The tribe of Naphtali represents one of the ten lost tribes of Israel from the twelve that constituted the people of Israel in biblical times, and each of the ten tribes bears the name of one of Jacob's sons or grandsons. Salathiel has a direct genealogical line to Naphtali, son of Jacob and Bilah (Genesis 30:8). Jacob is one of the three Abrahamic patriarchs, and Salathiel thus embodies a connection with the foundations of Judaism itself. Similarly, the name Salathiel, the Greek transliteration of Shealtiel, also appears in biblical texts. Referenced in 1 Chronicles 3:17–18 and in Matthew 1:2, Shealtiel was exiled to Babylon by Nebuchadnezzar II, and consequently regarded as the second Exilarch, or king-in-exile. Salathiel's names, then, speak to his royal and biblical ancestry,

---

[171] Milbank, *God and the Gothic*, p. 50.   [172] Croly, *Salathiel*, vol. 3, p. 416.

and highlight both his Jewishness and the physical space of Israel. Inheriting the princedom of Naphtali, Salathiel professes that the 'antiquity of possession gave a kind of hallowed and monumental interest to the soil',[173] but the novel concludes with Salathiel as a prince in exile from his Jewish homeland. This exilic state, however, implies a future return to Israel, and thus, through his wanderer, Croly signals the importance of Jewish foundations, of Israel and of the return of Jews to Israel.

While Croly constructs a distinctly *Jewish* wanderer, Salathiel is very much designed to bear witness to Christian truth and the idea that Christianity should supersede Judaism. Croly substantiates this claim through appeals to scripture and the inevitability of Armageddon. The original subtitle of the 1828 edition is 'A story of the Past, the Present, and the Future', exemplifying the structure of both the Wandering Jew story and Christianity as a religion that continually looks back to the Passion narrative, identifies the present moment as the Christian period of waiting, and anticipates a prophesied future state. Later editions modify the title. The 1901 edition, for example, bears the title 'Tarry thou till I come; or, Salathiel, the wandering Jew'. Taken from John 21:22, and recalling Paris's account of the Wandering Jew, 'Tarry thou till I come' appears as the first line of the novel, and the phrase is repeated throughout the narrative. This adapted title therefore accentuates the novel's implied scriptural foundations as it uses a phrase originally spoken by Jesus in the Gospel of John to explain Salathiel's punishment: he is doomed to wander until Christ's return.

Croly further incorporates details from the synoptic Gospels. Following the crucifixion – a moment of rupture that, in this novel, the Wandering Jew is partly responsible for – Salathiel observes that:

> The sun, which I had seen like a fiery buckler hanging over the city, was utterly gone. While I looked, the darkness deepened [...] I heard the hollow roar of an earthquake; the ground rose and heaved under our feet. I heard the crash of buildings, the fall of fragments of the hills, and, louder than both, the groan of the multitude. I caught my wife and child closer to my bosom. In the next moment, I felt the ground give way beneath me; a sulphurous vapour took away my breath.[174]

Conjuring his wanderer into the Passion narrative, Croly depicts the crucifixion as an event followed by darkness, earthquakes and the tearing of the temple veil, each being apocalyptic portents tied to the crucifixion as described in the synoptic Gospels (see Mark 33:15; Matt. 27:47; Luke 23:43–44). Mark 33:15, for example, states, 'there was a darkness over the whole land', while Matthew 27:51 recounts that 'the veil of the temple was rent in twain from the top to the

---

[173] Croly, *Salathiel*, vol. 2, p. 8.   [174] Croly, *Salathiel*, vol. 1, pp. 30, 37.

bottom and the earth did quake, and the rocks rent'. Notably, these portents are also common motifs in Jewish prophecy and apocalyptical literature. For example, in the Book of Amos, the prediction of an earthquake is connected with the omen of darkness: '"And it shall come to pass in that day," says the Lord God, "That I will make the sun go down at noon, And I will darken the earth in broad daylight"' (Amos 8:9). Considered to be prophetic omens or apocalyptic portents, the prominent inclusion of these motifs in Gospel accounts reveals the construction of a Christian narrative that aims to demonstrate the fulfilment of Jewish prophecy – but only in the context of a theology that recognises the legitimacy of the Christian Messiah. *Salathiel* imitates these canonical Gospel accounts and extends them; describing a range of sensory experiences, Salathiel writes, 'I looked, 'I heard' and 'I felt', giving a depth and a personal perspective to his narrative that is absent in Gospel accounts.

Although invoking similar moments of eschatological portents, *Salathiel* is distinct from its scriptural foundation through its use of first-person perspective. Narrating his story, Salathiel reveals that he is not only witness to the crucifixion, but complicit in it: 'I demanded instant execution of the sentence. – "Not a day of life must be given," I exclaimed; "not an hour: – death, on the instant; death!" My clamour was echoed by the roar of millions.'[175] As a moment of rupture, a transgressive act is central to Wandering Jew narratives in reframing original sin, the first transgression against God. While the crucifixion is presented as a substitutional sacrifice absolving original sin, the second transgression functions as a rebuke to God's sacrifice that merits punishment. *Salathiel* fleshes out this part of the myth, but filters it through a spectral Jewish eyewitness. In doing so, *Salathiel* embodies the antisemitic Christian concept that Jews are collectively guilty for the crucifixion of Christ:

> I saw at once the full guilt of my crime [...] Every fibre of my frame quivers, every drop of blood curdles, as I still hear the echo of the anathema that on the night of woe sprang from my furious lips, the self-pronounced ruin, the words of desolation, "HIS BLOOD BE UPON US, AND UPON OUR CHILDREN!"[176]

Salathiel is the exemplar of a 'Christ killer'. Again referencing scripture, *Salathiel* quotes Matthew 27:24–25: '"I am innocent of this man's blood," he [Pontius Pilate] said. "It is your responsibility!" All the people answered, "His blood is on us and on our children!"' The first-person pronoun in Salathiel's declaration of guilt links his role as witness to the crucifixion to an acknowledgement of his personal responsibility. This encounter is also experienced as

---

[175] Croly, *Salathiel*, vol. 1, p. 4.   [176] Croly, *Salathiel*, vol. 1, pp. 2–3.

a moment of Radcliffean horror that 'contracts, freezes, and nearly annihilates' Salathiel, and thus emphasises the enormity of his crime.[177] As his 'frame quivers' and 'every drop of blood curdles' he is suspended within this moment of rupture, and recalling it anew through his narrative returns him to relive the full sensory experience of this moment as if it is happening still, the horror of the act seeming frozen in time.

In condemning the Christian Messiah to death, Salathiel performs an act of unspeakable sacrilege that cannot be forgotten, but the novel suggests that responsibility and retribution for this crime is also shared and inherited by all Jewish people. A crowd of millions echo his demand for the death of Christ, and consequently the repercussions of this crime similarly fall on 'us': Salathiel's singular 'I' transforms into the plural 'us', and collective pronouns signify guilt that is shared and inherited by 'our children'. The inclusion of apocalyptic portents further serves to emphasise the enormity of this action and the idea of collective responsibility. Discussing crucifixion darkness within the Gospel of Matthew, Dale C. Allison notes the prevalent association of this motif with the judgement of God, further writing that anti-Judaic interpretations also connect the judgement of darkness at the crucifixion with the later destruction of the Jewish Temple in 70 CE.[178] Appealing to common apocalyptic motifs within Gospel accounts thus lays claims to Jewish prophecy, but as Croly employs the darkness portent in particular, it is further transformed into a judgement of God on Salathiel and the Jewish community collectively.

Salathiel begins with the Wandering Jew's transgression against Christ, describes his witnessing of the violent suffering and martyrdom of early Christians – which Salathiel reveals he is also partly responsible for – and then concludes with the destruction of the Second Temple in Jerusalem. In other reworkings of the Wandering Jew myth, including alchemical and Faustian versions, the 'punishment' that Jews are expected to suffer because of supposed transgressions against God are embodied in one figure (the wanderer himself), or occasionally bifurcated into two figures as in *Melmoth*. In *Salathiel*, though, the wanderer is initially punished as an individual transgressor before his punishment is shared with all Jewish people at the novel's conclusion, when the Temple is destroyed. This is significant, as the destruction of the Temple and the subsequent exile of Jews from Israel is considered within supersessionist theology to be a punishment by God, revealing 'the last and most wondrous sign, that marked the fate of rejected Israel'.[179]

---

[177] Radcliffe, 'On the Supernatural in Poetry', 145–52 (149).
[178] Allison, *Studies in Matthew*, p. 98.   [179] Croly, *Salathiel*, vol. 3, p. 398.

Mirroring the events that followed the crucifixion, Salathiel notes the chaos and darkness that followed the destruction of the Temple. Both moments can be viewed as transgressions against the body of God, whether the incarnated human body of Christ or the spiritual dwelling place of God within the Temple. In Judaism, the Temple is the dwelling place of God where 'God's "might and glory," could be "seen"'.[180] Paralleling its physical destruction, *Salathiel* depicts the spiritual ruin of the Temple:

> The vast portal opened, and from it marched a host, such as man had never seen before, such as man shall never see but once again; the guardian angels of the city of David! — they came forth glorious; but with woe in all their steps; the stars upon their helmets dim; their robes stained; tears flowing down their celestial beauty. 'Let us go hence,' was their song of sorrow. [...] Their chorus was heard, still magnificent and melancholy, when their splendour was diminished to the brightness of a star. Then the thunder roared again; the cloudy temple was scattered on the winds; and darkness, the omen of her grave, settled upon Jerusalem.[181]

Repeating apocalyptic portents, the spiritual destruction of the Temple and the repudiation of Israel forces all Jews to share the Wandering Jew's punishment, and encompasses the Christian period of waiting. Like the crucifixion, this moment is portrayed as monumental; yet while the crucifixion inspires horror, the destruction of the Temple and the departure of the heavenly host inspire terror. Radcliffe writes that terror 'expands the soul, and awakens the faculties to a high degree of life'.[182] While the horror of the crucifixion freezes Salathiel – and his immortal existence enacts this perpetual suspension in time – the sublime terror of the destruction of the Temple awakens Salathiel to the true gravity of his transgression and its consequences, and transfers his punishment to all who practice the Jewish faith.

Christian eschatology claims that Ancient Israel is superseded by Christianity, and the expected return of Christ is therefore tied to the physical land of Israel and the belief that the Temple, now standing like a Gothic ruin, will be rebuilt and become once more the dwelling place of God. Exploring this moment of rupture between Judaism and Christianity, Croly presents his readers with 'a new law, a new hope'.[183] Croly died before he could see the year he prophesied as the beginning of the End Times, but as we know, 1863 came and went without the apocalypse. Salathiel therefore joins the growing family of Wandering Jew spectres, including those conjured by Lewis, Godwin, Shelley and Maturin, who are still waiting for their death and Armageddon. Croly's novel does not

---

[180] Horowitz, *A Kabbalah and Jewish Mysticism Reader*, p. 51.
[181] Croly, *Salathiel*, vol. 3, pp. 399–400.
[182] Radcliffe, 'On the Supernatural in Poetry', p. 149.   [183] Croly, *Salathiel*, vol. 1, p. 243.

mark the end of the figure's appearances in fiction nor the end of Christian millenarianism, though, and both continue to be adapted and modified in relation to scriptural prophecy and popular interpretations of Christian eschatology. The Wandering Jew is a palimpsestic, spectralised, imagined Jew, and with each new conjuration, previous iterations can be glimpsed beneath the surface as each version adds distinct new layers whilst building on previous foundations. But whether the interpolated and expropriated parts relate to secular, alchemical, Faustian or theological contexts, at the heart of Wandering Jew myth are Christian anxieties tied to the religious narrative of transgression, rupture and the end of all things.

5 Conclusion: Gothic Legacies and Resurrections from *Dracula* to *Melmoth*

At the close of the nineteenth century, and long after the Romantics and Early Gothic writers had conjured their myriad versions of the Wandering Jew, the myth caught the attention of another writer, Bram Stoker. Poring over collections in the British library, Stoker's research led him to the Wandering Jew, and his fascination with this myth proved enduring. In his non-fiction publication, *Famous Imposters* (1910), he chronicled the history of the figure, recounting the 'immediate and lasting success' of George Croly's historical and biblical version, and further that the 'great vogue of *Salathiel* lasted some ten or more years, when the torch of the Wandering Jew was lighted by Eugene Sue'.[184] Sue was a prominent French author whose serialised Gothic novel *Le Juif Errant* or *The Wandering Jew* (1844–45) brought the myth into his present moment, adding new (antisemitic) layers through which Jews became associated with disease and an on-going cholera epidemic.[185] Stoker also ventured to revive the legend in a stage version, and H. L. Malchow notes that Stoker attempted to persuade his friend and celebrated actor Henry Irving to take up the role of the legendary wanderer.[186] Ultimately, Stoker's efforts were unsuccessful, but he never gave up his interest in the figure even as he turned his attention to other projects, including his 1897 novel *Dracula*. In *Dracula*, though, we can see new palimpsestic layers manifest in a new addition to the growing family of Wandering Jew spectres: the vampiric wanderer. Like the alchemist and Faustian versions of the Wandering Jew, the vampiric wanderer is not necessarily the Wandering Jew himself, but shares many connections with him.

---

[184] Stoker, *Famous Imposters*, pp. 114–5.
[185] Sue's version adapted the legend into a serial novel, and like his earlier *Les Mystères de Paris* or *The Mysteries of Paris*(1842–43), *The Wandering Jew* was one of the most popular.
[186] Malchow, *Gothic Images of Race in Nineteenth-Century Britain*, p. 138.

Along with his innumerable vampiric progeny, Dracula is a supernatural Other possessing an unnaturally long life as a societal outcast. His protracted existence affords him a long memory that allows him to recall historic events and figures as an eyewitness, while his recoiling from religious relics that testify to Christianity, such as crucifixes and Holy wafers, suggests that Dracula is damned. Moreover, though the circumstances of his vampiric origins are somewhat shrouded in mystery, his adversary Abraham Van Helsing avows that in life he was 'Soldier, statesman, and alchemist'.[187] However, Dracula is not just any alchemist, and as Van Helsing shares some of the research undertaken by his friend Arminius, of Buda-Pesth University, he invites his new associates (and the reader) to join him in the act of detective discovery. Chronicling Dracula's human pursuits, Van Helsing reveals that Dracula attended the Scholomance, a school of black magic in Romania that, according to folklore, is run by the Devil himself: 'The Draculas [...] had dealings with the Evil One. They learned his secrets in the Scholomance, amongst the mountains over Lake Hermanstadt, where the devil claims the tenth scholar as his due.'[188] Through his dealings with the Devil and alchemy, Dracula follows in the footsteps of the alchemical and Faustian wanderers that emerged from the Wandering Jew myth. Further imitating the original theological model of the myth that presents the wanderer's crime against Christ as a transgression against God, Dracula's embrace of the Devil and corresponding renunciation of the Christian God similarly serves as a warning against such sacrilegious transgressions.

Yet, this is also a story of hope, albeit one of hope deferred. While the Wandering Jew awaits Armageddon, Dracula is allowed to die, and his death is presented as a miracle that validates a theologically Christian perspective: 'That poor soul who has wrought all this misery is the saddest case of all. Just think what will be his joy when he too is destroyed in his worser part, that his better part may have spiritual immortality.'[189] Here, 'joy' recalls Luke 15:7 in which Christ declares that 'likewise joy shall be in heaven over one sinner that repenteth, more than over ninety and nine just persons, which need no repentance'. Though Stoker is not a clergyman, his novel does act as a sermon in fiction: even the worst sinners, including Dracula, can eventually find joy and salvation – if only they repent. Stoker thus picks up the torch passed on by Sue, his vampire manifesting a vast array of established Wandering Jew tropes and characteristics. Recalling Sue's wanderer in particular, Dracula is in part constructed as a foreign Other who threatens to bring disease and infection to Britain. In this, Stoker's novel reflects contemporary social anxieties surrounding Jewish immigration to London's East End, with Dracula being perceived as

---

[187] Stoker, *Dracula*, p. 321.   [188] Stoker, *Dracula*, p. 256.   [189] Stoker, *Dracula*, p. 328.

'dirty, swarming and overwhelmingly alien'.[190] Critics such as Jules Zanger, Ken Gelder and Carol Margaret Davison have all noted the similarities between the physical construction of Dracula and the racial and ethnic construction of the Jewish Other.[191] Underneath Dracula's monstrous, vampiric exterior is the spectre of an imagined Jewish Other: Dracula thus functions as another Wandering Jew figure – the vampiric wanderer – who is conjured to uphold Christian narratives.

The Gothic legacies of the Wandering Jew can be seen in the countless stories of alchemists, Faustian immortals and vampires that continue to be told. These stories appropriate elements from established traditions of the myth, interpolate new layers and forge palimpsestuous connections with previous and future versions, resulting in an ever growing family of spectral wanderers. To this day, the Wandering Jew still appears in fiction, though the figure has fallen out of fashion since the Romantic period as Gothic novelists have turned to other monsters, including the Wandering Jew's palimpsestic progeny. *Salathiel* may have been admired by Stoker, for example, but its popularity was short-lived. Attempts to revive interest in it – such as a 1901 American edition, republished under a new title *Tarry Thou Till I Come or, Salathiel, The Wandering Jew* and accompanied by twenty illustrations – were unsuccessful. This is perhaps due to overt Christian evangelism: the introduction to this edition provided by its religious publishers, Funk and Wagnalls, is antisemitic in its polemic, while discussion of the Wandering Jew myth ('an old, pathetic legend') is eschewed to instead preach Christian apologetics directly to the reader: 'Christ is coming, and that this coming is near at hand, is believed to-day by millions.'[192] Despite offering a new title, new images and a new introduction, this edition did not add anything to the Wandering Jew hypertext beyond re-emphasising, and perhaps overstating, the legend's Christian narrative. More recently, however, Sarah Perry's contemporary Gothic tale *Melmoth* (2018) has resurrected the myth, breathing new life into an old ghost.

Perry's third novel, *Melmoth,* is a book that haunts you. *Melmoth* takes the palimpsest of the Wandering Jew myth and Charles Robert Maturin's earlier novel *Melmoth the Wanderer*, to which the title of her novel directly alludes, and relocates it to a contemporary ghost story about a female Wandering Jew figure: Melmotte the Witness. This story follows Helen, whose life becomes consumed by the ghost haunting her. Following the death of Joseph Hoffman, an old man who frequented the same library that Helen and her friend, Dr Karel Pražan,

---

[190] Zanger, 'A Sympathetic Vibration', 33–4 (34).
[191] See Zanger's essay, 'A Sympathetic Vibration', Ken Gelder's *Reading the Vampire* (1994) and Davison's *Anti-Semitism and British Gothic Literature*, pp. 120–157.
[192] I. K. F., 'Introduction', pp. ix–xxx (p. ix).

regularly visited to work, Helen learns that this same ghost pursued them too. This ghost attached itself first to Hoffman, then Pražan and now Helen, and eventually Helen assumes the role of detective discoverer as she collates oral and written narratives relating to the spectre.

Perry's *Melmoth* is a 'homage' to *Melmoth the Wanderer* and, like Maturin's novel, is a multi-layered narrative comprising found documents and eyewitness accounts, with each narrative layer chronicling a catalogue of horrors connected to the mysterious Witness figure.[193] The story of Maturin's wanderer is filtered through the perspective of his descendant, John, who discovers various artefacts and is (along with the reader) the repository of stories told to him by an escaped Spanish monk. Helen fulfils the same function as John in Perry's novel. She is bequeathed by Pražan an array of primary sources that he has catalogued into a list of texts relating to their ghost, including 'The Ballad of Wheal Biding', 'The Hoffman Document' and 'The Testimony of Nameless and Hassan'. These texts allude to elements of the Wandering Jew tradition, such as the importance of ballads and oral storytelling. Maturin's novel also appears in this list, to which is added the note, 'the author's poverty, isolation, &c. – telling?? Had C. R. Maturin himself encountered the Witness?! Likely, if not probable'.[194] Adding Maturin as a principal character into a version of his own story adds a metafictional dimension to Perry's tale, as Maturin is transformed from author recounting a Wandering Jew story to a possible victim of the Wandering Jew. For Pražan, however, the haunting of Melmotte is too much for him to bear. He leaves his wife, his job and home country in the hope that he will no longer be haunted, and entrusts these documents to Helen – who soon finds herself besieged by a spectral woman in black.

While the Gothic authors discussed in this Element each added their own unique elements and characteristics to the legend, Perry's contemporary transformation is more radical. Through changing the gender of the wanderer, she exposes the male-centric nature of the myth and the many narratives it has inspired throughout history. Discussing nineteenth-century women authors such as Jane Austen, Mary Shelley and Emily Bronte, Sandra M. Gilbert and Susan Gubar argue that such writers both participated in and '"swerved" from the central sequences of male literary history, enacting a uniquely female process of revision and redefinition'.[195] Gilbert and Gubar further state that the literary works produced by these women can be considered to be palimpsestic because they are 'simultaneously conforming to and subverting patriarchal literary standards'.[196] In this way, established patriarchal literary

---

[193] Malcolm, 'I often say I was born in about 1890'.   [194] Perry, *Melmoth*, pp. 74–5.
[195] Gilbert and Gubar, *The Madwoman in the Attic*, p. 73.
[196] Gilbert and Gubar, *The Madwoman in the Attic*, p. 73.

traditions function like the vellum of palimpsestic manuscripts, and women's literary responses are simply the top most layer of this palimpsest. The Wandering Jew has generally been constructed as a male figure, but he has also been configured as the opposite of all that is Godly – and as such he embodies all that is Othered within Christian traditions. The Wanderer embodies Kruger's notion of the 'spectral Jew',[197] and the broader notion of a Jewish Other as imagined by Christianity has not always been male – and in fact has often been coded as the 'inversion' of the divine, Christian male (i.e. the Christian Messiah), a 'corrupt and polluted female body that, in the absence of divinity, was a likely vessel for evil'.[198]

Perry's transformation of the Wandering Jew into a woman thus exposes female layers already implicit in the myth, and this transformation also takes place in Perry's reconstitution of the apocryphal legend that surrounds her spectral Wanderer. The original story of the Wandering Jew and that of *Melmoth the Wanderer* hinges on transgression against God, where the male sinner is punished for insulting Christ. Though Maturin's novel is not a direct retelling of the Gospel, Perry returns to the Bible:

> You know, as your bible has taught you, that a company of women came to Jesus's tomb, and found it empty, and the stone rolled away, and right there in the garden they saw the risen son of God. But among them was one who later denied that she had ever seen the resurrected Christ. Because of it she is cursed to wander the earth without home or respite, until Christ comes again. So she is always watching, always seeking out everything that's most distressing and most wicked, in a world which is surpassingly wicked, and full of distress. In doing so she bears witness, where there is no witness, and hopes to achieve her salvation.[199]

Just as the Wandering Jew was retroactively inserted into Gospel accounts, so too Melmotte is placed ex post facto into Gospel accounts of the resurrection in order to challenge patriarchal traditions and interpretations of Christianity. The Bible was written by men for men, and Christianity is an enormously patriarchal religion. It is therefore notable that despite the male-dominated nature of the Bible, women are integral to the story of Christ. For example, according to the Gospel of John, the first person to whom Jesus reveals his true messianic identity is a Samaritan woman (John 4: 25–6); sisters Mary and Martha are important followers and friends of Jesus (John 11:1–44 and John 12: 1–8); and Mary Magdalene, known as the apostle to the apostles, is the woman to whom Jesus first appeared after his resurrection and whom he then sent to tell his

---

[197] Kruger, *The Spectral Jew*, p. 3.
[198] Gardenour, 'The Biology of Blood-Lust', 51–63 (55–6).   [199] Perry, *Melmoth*, p. 37.

disciples of this apparent miracle (John 20). While the Wandering Jew's supposed crime is that he insulted Christ, or that he is a Christ-killer, the crime of Melmotte is that she denied the resurrection and failed to testify, like the other women, to the evidence of Christianity. Joining the large array of Wandering Jew ghosts that are cursed to wander the earth until the End Times, Melmotte acts as witness to human horror in order to atone for her previous refusal to act as witness to God's miracles, seeking not a replacement but a companion to share in her struggle for salvation. Crucially, however, she also highlights how important and indivisible women are to Christian narratives and theologies of salvation.

Maturin's *Melmoth the Wanderer* is a sermon in fiction, and Perry's novel, too, reflects Christian theologies, although Perry's *Melmoth* manifests specifically feminist Christian thought. Perry has spoken about her upbringing in the confines of the Ebenezer Strict and Particular Baptist Chapel in Chelmsford: 'From a very young age I was reading the King James Bible, which is full of transgression and sin and anxiety and madness. I think it just formed my sensibility.'[200] Having since left the fundamentalist sect, and later the Church, a decision finally determined following the Church's opposition to same-sex marriage in 2007, Perry describes herself as 'post-religious' but not 'post-faith'.[201] Though Perry may not have conceived of *Melmoth* as a way to preach directly to her readers, as Maturin did, the Christian theologies that are at the heart of the Wandering Jew myth – including the idea that salvation can be found through God, while transgression against God will engender misery and even hellish punishment – can be glimpsed throughout her novel.

This is, however, not a patriarchal, male-centric Christianity but one in which women are placed at the centre. Claudia Setzer highlights the importance of feminist biblical scholarship in uncovering the significant role played by women in early Christian communities, noting that 'Nowhere is this clearer than in the resurrection narratives'.[202] In particular, Setzer highlights the role of Mary Magdalene as the first to uncover the empty tomb of Jesus as part of the indispensability of women's witness.[203] Women's ministry remains an often controversial topic of debate among many Christian communities. In 2007, for example, the Holy See of the Roman Catholic Church issued a decree stating that the attempted ordination of women would result in the automatic excommunication of both the woman and the priest undertaking this endeavour.[204] The role of women is similarly disputed in the Church of England: while the General

---

[200] Conroy, 'The female experience is not really something I can identify with'.
[201] Conroy, 'The female experience is not really something I can identify with'.
[202] Setzer, 'Excellent Women', 259–72 (259). [203] Setzer, 'Excellent Women', 259–69.
[204] Levada, 'General Decree regarding the delict of attempted sacred ordination of a woman'.

Synod of the Church of England passed a vote in 1992 to allow the ordination of women priests (and since 2005 there have been numerous votes relating to the ordination of Women Bishops), debates and successful votes allowing women ministry have been fiercely opposed by traditionalists within the Church of England. This has led to fractures within the Church, where some dioceses continue to ordain only men.[205]

Perry's decision to turn to the story of the resurrection and insert her Wandering Jew figure, Melmotte, into this narrative as a spectral foil to Mary Magdalene thus participates in this ongoing debate. *Melmoth* highlights the essential role of women's witness to Christianity, a role that can be traced back to Gospel accounts of the resurrection. Moreover, while the motivation of the original Wandering Jew's sin is often overlooked, the catalyst for Melmotte the Witness's dishonesty is rooted in the female experience: '"The reason she lied was because the women at the tomb weren't believed," Perry says. "So her whole curse is based on a woman who knew that men wouldn't believe her, and was then damned for it".'[206] Through a 'process of enfolding',[207] experiences of women throughout history, from the women chronicled in Gospel accounts as being present at the resurrection of Christ to women in our contemporary period, are enfolded into a story that might seem to relate only to men. Instead, as Perry uncovers, women, women's stories and women's experiences have always been indivisible from the ostensibly male story of the Wandering Jew and the theological narrative of Christianity that is at the heart of this legend.

Unlike the Wandering Jew texts of the Romantic period discussed in this Element, *Melmoth* was created in the continued aftermath of the Holocaust, and Perry's narrative calls attention to antisemitic traditions that the Wandering Jew myth has perpetuated (and even created). Perry avoids the explicit identification of the Wandering Jew as an ethnic and religious Other, an identity which is traditionally exploited to serve an antisemitic, Christian narrative. Instead, her spectre is primarily associated with her task of witnessing. Melmotte finds victims who have, like her, sinned; and as she watches their transgressions, she bides her time before seductively extending her hand for them to join her. One such victim is Joseph Hoffman. From his written confession that recounts his childhood in Prague, we learn that his jealousy of a family's possessions and his German pride taught to him by his father led Hoffman to expose them as Jews who have been living clandestinely. As a result of his actions, the house of this Jewish family is broken into, and Hoffman is told that, 'off they go to

---

[205] Cooke, '500 churches in the C of E still ban female priests'.
[206] Shapiro, 'Sarah Perry hopes the monster from her new novel is watching Harvey Weinstein'.
[207] Iğsız, 'Theorizing Palimpsests', 193–4.

Theresienstadt with the rest of their kind'.[208] Here we can consider the palimpsestuous enfolding of different readers along with Gerard Gennette's notion of a 'double "reception"'.[209] While the child Hoffman may not comprehend the significance of this destination, the adult Hoffman and indeed Perry's reader would be aware that the Theresienstadt ghetto was established by the Nazis as a forced labour camp that functioned as a stopping point on the way to extermination camps such as Auschwitz. Perry's transformation of the Wandering Jew legend thus further relocates the figure beyond antisemitic Christian apologetics; instead, through Hoffman's story, Perry's Melmotte holds a mirror up to historical antisemitism, forcing Hoffman, Helen and the reader to reflect on these horrors.

In this way, the reader of Perry's novel, and indeed the reader of every Wandering Jew hypertext, are revealed to have an important role to play. In the final line of Perry's novel, Melmotte directly addresses the reader, and it is as if her spectral hand reaches out from the pages to embrace them as a new victim: 'Oh my friend, my darling – won't you take my hand? I've been so lonely!'[210] Just as Hoffman and Helen are forced to confront their sins, so too the reader is invited to reflect on their own lives, and to question whether they have committed any actions deserving of an eternity of haunting punishment. However, the reader of a Wandering Jew hypertext is also a detective discoverer, and along with uncovering hidden clues and palimpsestuous connections that link such works with previous (and future) conjurations, the reader also brings their own interpretations to bear on the story. This is ultimately a Christian myth that has been employed to support and promote specifically Christian theologies. A contemporary reader might ask, then: can a radical transformation of the myth such as that found within Perry's *Melmoth* truly excise the antisemitic history of the Wandering Jew, who was often employed to promote not just Christian theology but Christian antisemitism? Within his stories, the Wandering Jew's spectral existence means that he can never be fully laid to rest – but for contemporary storytellers, perhaps it is time to find new ghosts to take his place.

---

[208] Perry, *Melmoth*, p. 129.   [209] Genette, *Palimpsests*, p. 374.   [210] Perry, *Melmoth*, p. 271.

Bibliography

Allison, Dale C., *Studies in Matthew: Interpretation Past and Present* (Grand Rapids, MI: Baker Academic, 2005).

Anonymous, 'Review of Melmoth, the Wanderer', *The Edinburgh Review*, 35.70 (1821), 353–62.

Anonymous, 'The Rev. George Croly, A.M.', *La Belle Assemblée*, vol. 8 (1828), 2–10.

Anonymous, 'The Rev. George Croly, LL.D.', *The Gentleman's Magazine and Historical Review*, 220 (January 1861), 104–7.

Anonymous, 'The Theatre', *Universal Magazine of Knowledge and Pleasure*, 100 (1797), 364–5.

Anonymous, 'The Wandering Jew', *La Belle Assemblée* vol. 6 (January 1809), 19–20.

Balzac, Honoré de, *Melmoth Reconciled*, trans. Ellen Marriage (Salt Lake City, UT: Project Gutenberg, 2016) [accessed via *Gutenberg*].

Baron-Wilson, Margaret, *The Life and Correspondence of M. G. Lewis*, 2 vols (London: Henry Colburn Publisher, 1939).

Behrendt, Stephen C., 'Introduction', in Stephen C. Behrendt (ed.), *Zastrozzi & St Irvyne* (Peterborough: Broadview Press, 2002), pp. 9–53.

Benstock, Shari, *Women of the Left Bank: Paris, 1900–1940* (Austin, TX: University of Texas Press, 1976).

Bergel, Giles, Howe, Christopher J., and Windram, Heather F., 'Lines of Succession in an English Ballad Tradition: The Publishing History and Textual Descent of The Wandering Jew's Chronicle', *Digital Scholarship in the Humanities*, 31.3 (2016), 540–62.

Bicheno, James, *Signs of the Times; or the Overthrow of the Papal Tyranny in France* (London: Parsons, 1793).

Byron, Lord George Gordon, 'Letter 377: To Mr Murray', in Thomas Moore (ed.), *The Works of Lord Byron: Letters and Journals* (London: John Murray, 1832), vol. 4, pp. 320–1.

Cohausen, Johann Heinrich, *Hermippus Redivivus* (Dublin: Margt. Rhames, 1744).

Coleridge, Samuel Taylor, *Biographia Literaria; or Biographical Sketches of My Literary Life and Opinions*, 2 vols. (London: Rest Fenner, 1817).

Coleridge, Samuel Taylor, 'The Blasphemy of The Monk', in Victor Sage (ed.), *The Gothick Novel: A Casebook* (London: Macmillan, 1991), pp. 39–43.

Coleridge, Samuel Taylor, 'The Rime of the Ancient Mariner', in Stanley Applebaum (ed.), *The Rime of the Ancient Mariner and Other Poems* (New York: Dover, 1992), pp. 5–23.

Colosimo, Jennifer Driscoll, 'Schiller and the Gothic – Reception and Reality', in Jeffrey L. High, Nicholas Martin and Norbert Oellers (eds.), *Who Is Schiller Now: Essays on His Reception and Significance* (New York: Camden House, 2011), pp. 287–301.

Conger, Syndy M., *Matthew G. Lewis, Charles Robert Maturin and the Germans: An Interpretive Study of the Influence of German Literature on Two Gothic Novel* (Salzburg: Institut für Englische Sprache und Literatur, Universität Salzburg, 1976).

Conroy, Catherine, '"The female experience is not really something I can identify with": Sarah Perry discusses faith, writing, gender and illness as more than a metaphor', *The Irish Times* (11 July 2017) www.irishtimes.com/culture/books/the-female-experience-is-not-really-something-i-can-identify-with-1.3148519 [Date accesses: 1 July 2023].

Cooke, Felicity, '"500 churches in the C of E still ban female priests": Dioceses Commission Review sparks comment in The Sunday Times', *WATCH* (24 May 2019) womenandthechurch.org/news/500-churches-in-the-c-of-e-still-ban-female-priests-dioceses-commission-review-sparks-comment-in-the-sunday-times/ [Accessed: 20 July 2023].

Croix, G. E. M. de Ste., 'Why Were the Early Christians Persecuted?', *Past & Present*, 26 (1963), 6–38.

Croly, George, 'Preface', in *Salathiel: A Story of the Past, the Present, and the Future*, 3 vols (London: Henry Colburn, 1828), vol. 1, pp. v–vii.

Croly, George, *Salathiel: A Story of the Past, the Present, and the Future*, 3 vols (London: Henry Colburn, 1828).

Croly, George, *The Apocalypse of St John: Or Prophecy of the Rise, Progress, and Fall of the Church of Rome; the Inquisition; the Revolution of France; the Universal War; and the Final Triumph of Christianity. Being a New Interpretation* (London: C. & J. Rivington, 1827).

Crome, Andrew, *Christian Zionism and English National Identity, 1600–1850* (London: Palgrave Macmillan, 2018).

Davison, Carol Margaret, *Anti-Semitism and British Gothic Literature* (New York: Palgrave Macmillan, 2004).

Derrida, Jacques, *Specters of Marx: The State of the Debt, the Work of Mourning and the New International*, trans. Peggy Kamuf (London: Routledge Classics, 2006).

Dillon, Sarah, *The Palimpsest: Literature, Criticism, Theory* (London: Bloomsbury, 2007).

Dobell, Bertram, 'Introduction', in Betram Dobell (ed.), *The Wandering Jew* (London: Reeves and Turner, 1887), pp. xiii–xxxii.

Doney, Malcolm, '"I often say I was born in about 1890": Sarah Perry, raised a Strict Baptist, talks to Malcolm Doney', *Church Times* (30 November 2018). www.churchtimes.co.uk/articles/2018/30-november/features/features/i-often-say-i-was-born-in-about-1890 [Accessed: 1 July 2023].

Eagleton, Terry, *Heathcliff and the Great Hunger: Studies in Irish Culture* (London: Verso, 1995).

Eisner, Lotte H., *The Haunted Screen: Expressionism in the German Cinema and the Influence of Max Reinhardt* (Berkeley, CA: University of California Press, 2008).

Edelmann, R., 'Ahasuerus, The Wandering Jew: Origin and Background', in Galit Hasan-Rokem and Alan Dundes (eds.), *The Wandering Jew: Essays in the Interpretation of a Christian Legend* (Bloomington, IN: Indiana University Press, 1986), pp. 1–10.

Funk, Isaac Kaufmann, 'Introduction', in *Tarry Thou Till I Come or, Salathiel, The Wandering Jew* (New York: Grosset & Dunlap, 1901), pp. ix–xxx.

Esq, S., R., *The New Monk*, 3 vols (London: Minerva Press, 1798).

Flammel, Nicholas, *Alchemical Hieroglyphics*, trans. Eirenaeus Orandus (New Jersey, NJ: Heptangle Books, 1980).

Frank, Frederick S., *The First Gothics: A Critical Guide to the English Gothic Novel* (London: Garland, 1987).

Gardenour, Brenda, 'The Biology of Blood-Lust: Medieval Medicine, Theology, and the Vampire Jew', *Film & History, An Interdisciplinary Journal of Film and Television Studies*, 41.2 (2011), 51–63.

Genette, Gérard, *Palimpsests: Literature in the Second Degree*, trans. Channa Newman and Claude Doubinsky (Lincoln, NE: University of Nebraska Press, 1997).

Gilbert, Sandra M. and Gubar, Susan, *The Madwoman in the Attic : The Woman Writer and the Nineteenth-Century Literary Imagination* (New Haven, CT: Yale University Press, 2020).

Ginzberg, Louis, *The Legends of the Jews*, trans. Henrietta Szold (Philadelphia, PA: The Jewish Publication Society of America, 1937).

Godwin, William, *Lives of the Necromancers* (London: Frederick J Mason, 1834).

Godwin, William, *St Leon; A Tale of the Sixteenth Century*, ed. William Brewer (Plymouth: Broadview Editions, 2006).

Goethe, Johann Wolfgang von, *Faust: A Tragedy in Two Parts*, trans. Thomas Wayne (New York: Algora, 2016).

Goethe, Johann Wolfgang von, *The Autobiography of Goethe: Truth and Poetry: From My Own Life*, trans. A. J. W. Morrison (London: Henry G. Bohn, 1949).

Hasan-Rokem, Galit, 'The Enigma of a Name', *The Jewish Quarterly Review*, 100.4 (2010), 544–50.

Hogle, Jerrold E., 'Introduction', in Jerrold E. Hogle (ed.), *The Cambridge Companion to Gothic Fiction* (Cambridge: Cambridge University Press, 2006), pp. 1–20.

Horowitz, Daniel M., *A Kabbalah and Jewish Mysticism Reader* (Philadelphia, PA: The Jewish Publication Society, 2016).

Iğsız, Aslı, 'Theorizing Palimpsests: Unfolding Pasts into the Present', *History of the Present*, 11.2 (October: 2021), 192–208.

Isaac-Edersheim, E., 'Ahasver: A Mythic Image of the Jew', in Galit Hasan-Rokem and Alan Dundes (eds.), *The Wandering Jew: Essays in the Interpretation of a Christian Legend* (Bloomington, IN: Indiana University Press, 1986), pp. 195–210.

Kruger, Steven F., *The Spectral Jew: Conversion and Embodiment in Medieval Europe* (Minneapolis, MN: University of Minnesota Press, 2006).

Lampert-Weissig, Lisa, 'The Transnational Wandering Jew and the Medieval English Nation', *Literature Compass*, 13.12 (2016), 771–83.

Levada, William Cardinal, 'General Decree regarding the delict of attempted sacred ordination of a woman', *Congregation for the Doctrine of the Faith* (19 December 2007) www.vatican.va/roman_curia/congregations/cfaith/documents/rc_con_cfaith_doc_20071219_attentata-ord-donna_en.html [Accessed: 20 July 2023].

Lewis, Matthew, *The Monk*, ed. Howard Anderson (Oxford: Oxford University Press, 2008).

Lovecraft, Howard Phillips, *Supernatural Horror in Literature* (New York: Dover, 1973).

Malchow, Howard L., *Gothic Images of Race in Nineteenth-Century Britain* (California, CA: Stanford University Press, 1996).

Marana, Giovanni Paolo, *The Second Volume of Letters Writ by a Turkish Spy, Who Lived Fiver and Forty Years, Undiscover'd, at Paris*, 5th ed., trans. Robert Midgley and William Bradshaw (London: J. Leake, 1702).

Marlowe, Christopher, *Doctor Faustus*, ed. Roma Gill (London: The New Mermaids, 1965).

Maturin, Charles, *Melmoth the Wanderer*, ed. 1820 (Oxford: Oxford University Press, 2008).

Maturin, Charles, 'Preface', in Douglas Grant (ed.), *Melmoth the Wanderer* (Oxford: Oxford University Press, 2008), pp. 5–6.

Maturin, Charles, *Sermons* (Edinburgh: Archibald Constable, 1819).

Medwin, Thomas, 'Preface', in *Ahasuerus, The Wanderer: A Dramatic Legend* (London: G. and W. B. Whittaker, 1823).

Medwin, Thomas, *The Life of Percy Bysshe Shelley*, 2 vols (London: Thomas Cautley Newby, 1847).

Milbank, Alison, *God and the Gothic: Religion, Romance, and Reality in the English Literary Tradition* (Oxford: Oxford University Press, 2018).

Mulvey-Roberts, Marie, *Gothic Immortals: The Fiction of the Brotherhood of the Rosy Cross* (London: Routledge, 1990).

Nicoll, Allardyce, *A History of Early Nineteenth-Century Drama: 1800–1850*, 2 vols (Cambridge: Cambridge University Press, 1930).

O'Sullivan, Keith M. C., 'His Dark Ingredients: The Viscous Palimpsest of Charles Maturin's Melmoth the Wanderer', *Gothic Studies*, 18.2 (2016), 74–85.

Paris, Matthew, *Flowers of History*, 4 vols, trans. J. A. Giles (Felinfach: Llanerch, 1996), vol. 2.

Perry, Sarah, *Melmoth* (London: Serpent's Tail, 2018).

Potter, Franz J., *Gothic Chapbooks, Bluebooks and Shilling Shockers, 1797–1830* (Cardiff: University of Wales Press, 2021).

Quincey, Thomas de, 'The Palimpsest', in Quincey, Thomas de (ed.), *Blackwood's Edinburgh Magazine*, vol. 57 (Edinburgh: William Blackwood & Sons, June 1845), pp. 739–743.

Radcliffe, Ann, 'On the Supernatural in Poetry: By the Late Mrs. Radcliffe', *The New Monthly Magazine and Literary Journal*, 1 (1826), 145–52.

Railo, Eino, *The Haunted Castle: A Study of the Elements of English Romanticism* (New York: Routledge, 2018).

Ragaz, Sharon, 'Maturin, Archibald Constable, and the Publication of Melmoth the Wanderer', *The Review of English Studies*, 57.230 (2006) 359–73.

Ragussis, Michael, *Figures of Conversion: "The Jewish Question" & English National Identity* (Durham, NC: Duke University Press, 1995).

Reynolds, George W. M., 'The Wandering Jew', *Reynolds's Miscellany*, 11.281 (1853), 280.

Roos, Anna Marie, 'Johann Heinrich Cohausen (1665–1750), Salt Iatrochemistry, and Theories of Longevity in his Satire, Hermippus Redivivus (1742)', *Medical History*, 51 (2007), 181–200.

Rubinstein, William D., *A History of the Jews in the English-Speaking World: Great Britain* (London: Macmillan Press, 1996).

Sage, Victor, *The Gothic Novel* (London: Macmillan Press, 1991).

Schubart, Christian Friedrich Daniel, '"The Eternal Jew: A Lyrical Rhapsody" (1784)', trans. Sandra Hoenle, in D. L. Macdonald and Kathleen Scherf (eds.), *The Monk* (Peterborough: Broadview Press, 2004), pp. 379–82.

Scrivener, Michael, 'Reading Shelley's Ahasuerus and Jewish Orations: Jewish Representation in the Regency', *Keats-Shelley Journal*, 61 (2012), 133–8.

Scult, Mel, *Millennial Expectations And Jewish Liberties* (The Netherlands: Leiden, 1978).

Sermon, Maturin's, 'On the Death of Lord Nelson' where he appeals to the Gothic threat of the anti-Christ in his hellfire sermon warning against nationalism, *Sermons* (1819), pp. 49–50.

Setzer, Claudia, 'Excellent Women: Female Witness to the Resurrection', *Journal of Biblical Literature*, 116.2 (1997) 259–272.

Shapiro, Lila, 'Sarah Perry hopes the monster from her new novel is watching Harvey Weinstein', *Vulture* (22 October 2022) www.vulture.com/2018/10/sarah-perry-on-her-gothic-novel-melmoth-and-metoo.html [Accessed: 1 July 2023].

Shelley, Percy Bysshe, *The Wandering Jew* (London: Reeves and Turner, 1887).

Shelley, Percy Bysshe, 'St Irvyne', in Stephen C. Behrendt (ed.), *Zastrozzi & St Irvyne* (Lancaster: Broadview Press, 2002), pp. 159–252.

Shelley, Percy Bysshe and Shelly, Elizabeth, 'Gasta; or, The Avenging Demon!!!', in Richard Garnett (ed.), *Original Poetry: By Victor and Cazire* (London: John Lane, 1898), pp. 50–62.

Stephen, Leslie, *Dictionary Of National Biography*, 63 vols (London: Smith, Elder, 1888), vol. 13.

Stoker, Bram, *Dracula*, ed. Maurice Hindle (London: Penguin Classics, 2003).

Stoker, Bram, *Famous Imposters* (New York: Sturgis & Walton, 1910).

Tichelaar, Tyler R., *The Gothic Wanderer: From Transgression to Redemption* (Ann Arbor, MI: Modern History Press, 2012).

The Wandering Jew's Chronicle (ed.), Giles Bergel, Bodleian Library, wjc.bodleian.ox.ac.uk/index.html [Accessed: 10 December 2019].

Tamara Tinker, *The Impiety of Ahasuerus: Percy Shelley's Wandering Jew* (Charleston, SC: BookSurge, 2012).

Thomson, Heidi, 'Wordsworth's 'Song for the Wandering Jew' as a Poem for Coleridge', *Romanticism*, 21.1 (2015) 37–47.

Thorslev, Jr., Larsen, Peter, *The Byronic Hero: Types and Prototypes* (Minneapolis, MN: University of Minnesota Press, 1962).

Walpole, Horace, 'Preface to the First Edition', in W. S. Lewis (ed.), *The Castle of Otranto* (Oxford: Oxford University Press, 2008), pp. 5–8.

Wheatley, Kim, '"Strange Forms": Percy Bysshe Shelley's *Wandering Jew* and *St Irvyne*', *Keats-Shelley Journal*, 65 (2016) 70–88.

Zanger, Jules, 'A Sympathetic Vibration: Dracula and the Jews', *English Literature in Transition, 1880–1920*, 34.1 (1991), 33–4.

Cambridge Elements ⁼

The Gothic

Dale Townshend
Manchester Metropolitan University
Dale Townshend is Professor of Gothic Literature in the Manchester Centre for Gothic Studies, Manchester Metropolitan University.

Angela Wright
University of Sheffield
Angela Wright is Professor of Romantic Literature in the School of English at the University of Sheffield and co-director of its Centre for the History of the Gothic.

Advisory Board
Enrique Ajuria Ibarra, *Universidad de las Américas, Puebla, Mexico*
Katarzyna Ancuta, *Chulalongkorn University, Thailand*
Fred Botting, *University of Kingston, UK*
Carol Margaret Davison, *University of Windsor, Ontario, Canada*
Rebecca Duncan, *Linnaeus University, Sweden*
Jerrold E. Hogle, *Emeritus, University of Arizona*
Mark Jancovich, *University of East Anglia, UK*
Dawn Keetley, *Lehigh University, USA*
Roger Luckhurst, *Birkbeck College, University of London, UK*
Eric Parisot, *Flinders University, Australia*
Andrew Smith, *University of Sheffield, UK*

About the Series
Seeking to publish short, research-led yet accessible studies of the foundational 'elements' within Gothic Studies as well as showcasing new and emergent lines of scholarly enquiry, this innovative series brings to a range of specialist and non-specialist readers some of the most exciting developments in recent Gothic scholarship.

Cambridge Elements ≡

The Gothic

Elements in the Series

Gothic Voices: The Vococentric Soundworld of Gothic Writing
Matt Foley

Mary Robinson and the Gothic
Jerrold E. Hogle.

Folk Gothic
Dawn Keetley

The Last Man and Gothic Sympathy
Michael Cameron

Democracy and the American Gothic
Michael J. Blouin

Dickens and the Gothic
Andrew Smith

Contemporary Body Horror
Xavier Aldana Reyes

The Music of the Gothic: 1789–1820
Emma McEvoy

African American Gothic in the Era of Black Lives Matter
Maisha Wester

The Eternal Wanderer: Christian Negotiations in the Gothic Mode
Mary Going

A full series listing is available at: www.cambridge.org/GOTH

www.ingramcontent.com/pod-product-compliance
Ingram Content Group UK Ltd.
Pitfield, Milton Keynes, MK11 3LW, UK
UKHW020751060225
454697UK00024B/156